The Copper Room

The Copper Room
Henry Melton

Wire Rim Books
Hutto, Texas

WRB

Printing History
First Edition: November 2011
ISBN 978-1-935236-33-7

ePub ISBN 978-1-935236-34-4
Kindle ISBN 978-1-935236-35-1

Website of Henry Melton
www.HenryMelton.com

Cover art © 2011 Fred Perry and Wes Hartman

Printed in the United States of America

Wire Rim Books
www.wirerimbooks.com

Special thanks to my beta-readers who have done a great job pointing out numerous mistakes in the early version: Debra and Jonathan Andrews, Joe Blackmon, Jim Dunn, Linda Elliott, Mike Lynch, Mary Ann Melton, Mary Solomon, Tom Stock, Leona Urban, and Nick Wall

Dedicated to my little sister Martha Barnett. She crept into the pages of several books over the past few years as an inspiration for many characters. And she probabaly will again.

Table of Contents

Year Zero

"Just two weeks, Jereomy, two weeks help, and I'll guarantee that you'll have more than enough time to get everything done by graduation."

Jerry Harris frowned at his phone, considering Uncle Greg's request. Not that he wasn't a great guy—one of his favorite relatives. Ordinarily he wouldn't have objected at all to a little construction job on the side, but basketball season was in full swing, and everyone was saying that the home stretch in his senior year was going to be a madhouse.

But Uncle Greg had bought him his laptop, and the guy never welched on their deals.

"Okay. I'll do it. You make sure Mom is cool with it."

...

Greg Montain's house was about 20 miles east, just off Highway 61 in the little town of Canton, Missouri, right on the river. It wasn't far, but it was out of town. His parents would have to okay it.

His mother had her reservations when he brought it up that evening. "You know that your scholarship results are likely to hang on a good class standing. You can't let your grades slip."

She called her brother and they talked. He must have been a good salesman, because after a few minutes, she gave her blessing. "Do a good job," she said.

. . .

Uncle Greg's house looked like a wreck as he drove up a little past five on Thursday. The little guest bedroom in the rear was being rebuilt.

Greg's shirt was covered in white streaks as he waved him in. "Glad to see you, boy. Grab a hammer. We're taking out all the sheetrock."

"Are you putting up new paneling on the walls?"

He smiled. "New walls, new floor, new ceiling. We'll be taking out the windows, and the air duct. Totally new wiring and I'm replacing the door with something new."

Jerry put his hammer through the wallboard with a will. "Are you building a lab?" The destruction was fun.

Greg was a scientist, and his uncle had given him chemistry sets, microscopes and science fiction books all his life. A couple of Greg's inventions had gone big time and he no longer worked for the university down in St. Louis.

The man had a gleeful look in his eyes. "Something like that. I'm running an experiment, and I'd appreciate it if you kept quiet about it. As far as anyone else is concerned, I'm just remodeling."

"Gotcha."

. . .

Friday, he'd only managed a couple of hours work, with basketball making its own demands on his time and it was dark by the time he quit. His clothes were covered in chalky powder. The trailer-sized metal trash bin in the driveway was nearly full with stripped out wall and ceiling finishings.

I don't want to get this stuff in my Jeep. He turned on the headlights and dusted his jeans by slapping at the worst of the white patches. He froze when he saw a girl watching his antics from the next house over. She put her hand over her mouth to hide a laugh. He nodded and lifted his fingers in a little wave. She waved back and then vanished from the window.

...

He met her on Saturday.

"Your name is 'Germ'?" she asked suspiciously.

Her name was Lil Nyson, and she wore a red sweatshirt labeled with Canton Tigers. The jacket he usually wore had the big H of the Highland High School on it.

"Actually, it's J-E-R-M. And that's what my family calls me. I'd prefer, Jerry. Dad wanted a Bible name and chose Jeremiah. Mom had other ideas and filled in the birth certificate with the spelling J-E-R-E-O-M-Y. My little brother called me Jerm and it stuck. Unfortunate, but I can't get my family to get used to anything different."

She had brought tea over while he was sawing support beams in the front yard. Greg was inside laying out copper sheets on the foundation slab. Jerry was fascinated by the process, but that was part of what he was supposed to keep secret, and he was happy to spend a few minutes talking to Lil instead.

...

The room gradually took shape. Thick copper sheeting covered the floors and walls. New wooden pillars supported a copper ceiling. Greg welded all the seams, making the doorway the only opening to the room.

"It will be airtight, once I install the new door, but that's really beside the point, having the room entirely enclosed in a conductive barrier makes it a Faraday Cage. Radio waves can't get through. Nothing electromagnetic gets through." But he didn't say why that was important.

The door was iron. It took the two of them plus the delivery guys to move the door into the hallway on rollers. Greg had hydraulic jacks to lift it in place.

"It looks like a bank vault door."

Greg shook his head as they eased the black slab carefully up to the frame that he'd already built into the copper. There was a seal all the way around, and people had to step over the bottom rim to get inside.

"It's an industrial hatch. Designed for airtight chambers and the like. And it's conductive, like the copper."

Mated to the seal and balanced on the large hinges, the door moved easily, swinging into the room. Sealing it closed required a lever on the inside that pressed the door into the surrounding metal guides.

"I'm going to need a air supply for this place," Greg muttered. They had closed the door and checked the electrical connection with the walls.

Maybe it was just his imagination, but Jerry could feel the air begin to get stale. "And a lighting system. Unless you want to work by flashlight." They had ripped out the wall sockets and overhead lights with the rest of the old wallboard. The copper colored walls looked strange by the blue-LED light of his flashlight.

Uncle Greg moved the latching lever and a blast of fresh air came in with the daylight as he pulled the door open.

"That's my job. And I can handle it myself. Thanks for all your help."

Jerry was happy to get paid, but as he drove away, he looked unsuccessfully for Lil, sorry to be leaving.

. . .

A few weeks later, basketball, a math test, and two essays were coming due all at once. He remembered Uncle Greg's cryptic promise and called him.

"I was wondering if I could come over and study at your house." And if he managed to say hello to the neighbor, that'd be a plus.

Greg thought a moment and then said, "You're right, I did say I'd help. So here's what you need to do."

Jerry loaded his books into the car and then concentrated on the game as Greg suggested. He'd do the studying later.

. . .

It was a loud game with the traditional Canton rivals, and he did well, scoring twenty points himself. And that was in spite of discovering Lil was a cheerleader for the opposing team.

He sought her out when the game ended—just to say "hi".

"I'm even headed over to my uncle's house to study as soon as I change. "

"Oh, could you drop me off at my house? There's a usual get-together after games. That would let me change and pick up my car and not have to bum a ride home after," she asked.

"Sure."

She invited him to the party, as they drove, but the pile of books and the long night of studying he faced made it impossible.

He let her out and she skipped up her sidewalk, white pom-poms on her shoes dancing. As she vanished out of sight, he sighed. Studying was not what he wanted to do with his time.

But his grade point average was important, and the final race for class standings and the corresponding scholarship dollars had to come first. Making it into a great school had been a dream, but one that was fast fading as he learned how much that would cost.

Greg was waiting for him, a bag of burgers and fries fresh from Saints Avenue Cafe in his hand.

"Great. I'm starved."

"Not just yet." Greg set the bag down the floor and walked Jerry into the copper room. There were changes. A bed, chair and study table had been added, all lit from a large bank of batteries and LED track lighting. There were also some air tanks with other apparatus.

The standing grandfather clock just visible out the doorway began its hourly chimes. "Just in time."

Greg closed the massive door and turned a dial on the wall and flipped a switch. The muffled chime of the clock abruptly stopped.

"What's up?"

Greg gestured to the table.

"Jeremy, have a seat. I need to explain a few things."

His stomach rumbled, and he thought about the burgers outside getting cold, but he listened.

Greg pointed at the display panel mounted on the wall beside the door. "This dial sets the time rate." Jerry could see that it was set at 100X, but the scale went much farther. The actual numbers in the scale were hand lettered.

Greg nodded at his puzzled look. "I had to calibrate this manually.

"Time is flowing at a different rate inside the copper box. We are aging a hundred times faster than the outside."

Jerry thought about it with understandable suspicion, but after all, it was Uncle Greg. "You mean like that story with the gold pocket watch?" It was one of the books he had given him a few years back.

"Almost. Yes, the rest of the world seems frozen, but we can't really interact with it like they could in the John D. McDonald book. We have to stay within the protective shield of the walls. And at a one hundred times time rate, you'd never be able to move through the air, or breathe for that matter."

"Oh," he said, a little disappointed.

Greg said, "But one thing it can do is give you lots of time to study. You can come in here and shut out the world. At this rate, an hour and a half would pass by and when you shut it down, it would be less than a minute. Plenty of time to study, take a nap, and study some more. Plus, there's no outside distractions. No Internet. No TV unless you bring a recording in with you.

"And when you're done, the rest of your life hasn't left you behind." Greg flipped the switch on the wall. The clock chime picked up where it had stopped and when they opened the door, the fries were still hot.

. . .

Greg showed him the controls while Jerry munched on the fries and tried to absorb it all.

"The difference between a hundred and a thousand is minimal. You'll only save a few real world seconds by pushing the dial all the way over. The real limit is how long the batteries and air supply hold out. Which should be about two days. I've got a carbon dioxide scrubber to keep the air fresh. When the door is closed, it's like you're in a spaceship, with your own enclosed life support. There's even a portable toilet, but I'd recommend just turning off the switch and using the real bathroom outside. You can go right back in. You don't have to do the study session all in one go."

"What's this other one?" To the side of the controls Greg was demonstrating, there was a nearly identical set with its own large dial.

"Don't touch that. The time distortion works both ways. You can slow down your time as well, but it's very dangerous."

"Why?"

Uncle Greg grimaced. "Just think about it. Suppose you sped up the outside world a hundred times and then took a nap. You'd fail out of school. The police would be looking for you as a missing person. And people like me would be investigated for kidnapping or murder. And what's worse is that even if I told everyone the truth, I wouldn't be able to rescue you. The controls are inside, they have to be, and the whole room would be a block of frozen time that I wouldn't be able to open."

"Are you sure it works?" Jerry frowned at the innocent-looking dial.

"Yes, I just started trying to calibrate it. You can see this mark." He pointed to a dot just a couple of ticks off the pin. "That's one minute inside to one hour outside. The next tick after that took me three days in thirty seconds. Luckily, I'm a bachelor and can afford to vanish for three days, but it was enough to scare me off for a while. I'm thinking about adding an automated timer for this, so I can turn the distortion on for only a fraction of a second. Manual operations are just too slow and imprecise."

Greg pointed back at the first set of controls. "But these are fine. You can't get in much trouble this way. Are you ready to start your study session?"

. . .

And it was fine. Greg left him inside with his books, and after a nice long nap, he was able to get to work on his first essay. Maybe ten hours later, with plenty of time to doze and study and think, he finished both essays and was confident he'd be ready for the math test. He snapped off the switch and opened the door. Greg was just outside.

"How long was I?"

"Maybe a minute." He pointed at the clock, still ticking away with the minute hand just barely past the hour.

"Wow. This is really great. Can I use it again? My calendar is really packed."

"Sure, if I can get your help with some testing from time to time. As you can imagine, this is really hush-hush. You're the only one who knows about it. I'm not even sure what to do with the discovery."

"You should be able to make a bundle. I'd pay to have a study room in my house."

"Sure. But it could be dangerous too. How long has it been since you were here last?"

"Hmm. Maybe a month."

"For me, it's been nearly a year. Certainly, it made sense to extend my time working on the chamber, but if I kept it up, I'd grow old and die well before my time."

"But not really, right? You live the same number of seconds."

"Right, but what would your mother think, if I showed up at your house with gray hair and wrinkles? It's a trade-off. And it's something I'm just learning to deal with."

Jerry grinned. "Just use the other dial and skip through some of the boring days. Make it balance out."

. . .

Walking back to his car, it felt like the next day, although he must have been inside only a few minutes. Lil came out, dressed in slacks and a jacket.

8

"Hey, is that invite still open?" he asked.

"I thought you had to study."

"It was easier than I thought."

"Sure, come on. I'd love to have you along."

. . .

The short after-game party was fun, even as one of the opposing team's players. Lil was intent on introducing him around to her friends, but she was exhausted long before he was, and it was a school day.

He went home, his head churning with the ideas of what was possible with the copper room. And with thoughts of Lil.

. . .

The next day was horrible. He hadn't slept well, and the bonus hours messed up his body clock. He nearly fell asleep during the math test.

"Uncle Greg?" he spoke into his phone.

"Yes? Is there a problem?"

"I think I've got jet lag."

"Oops. I had that. I forgot to warn you. Come on by."

He arrived after school.

"You had an extra ten hours. It's five now. Do you want to skip ahead to 3AM or get another fourteen hours of rest and study?"

Jerry shook his head. "I don't think I want to drag home at 3AM, even if you call and try to explain. I've got tons of reading to catch up with. I'll study."

He did it in two sessions, with a break between when Greg took him out for a steak. By six, he was back on his regular body clock, rested, and caught up on studies.

"I can see how this could get addicting."

Greg nodded with a smile. "Maybe I should cut you off."

"Cut me off after I graduate. There just aren't enough hours in the day right now."

...

It was Friday night, his studies were caught up and he was rested. He called Lil. "Take in a movie?"

"Don't you ever study?"

"Hey, it's Friday. I can study over the weekend."

She gave in. She had to get her parents' permission to make the drive to Quincy across the river, but Jerry gave all the proper assurances. Movie, popcorn, and then they talked. She had her own college worries. Her parents were quite pleased with the idea of her attending Culver-Stockton college just a few blocks away. But as much as she loved her home town, the idea of seeing more of the world appealed to her.

He returned her home, just barely making her deadline.

They paused on the front porch. Lil smiled. "I wish we had more time." She kissed him at the door and went in.

He lingered for a moment, then before her parents got worried, walked back to the Jeep.

More time. That was a thought. More time with Lil.

...

Back at school, he got a few ribbing remarks about dating the enemy, but he didn't care.

In spite of Uncle Greg's offers, he refrained from begging more study breaks. It was tempting, considering that he was there at Lil's house several times a week, either picking her up or dropping her off. Using the copper room meant study time away from her, since he had to keep the secret.

Her parents gave him the careful eye, but once he went with them to an Easter presentation at their church where Lil was singing, he must have passed their test. After that, they greeting him with a smile when he showed up.

Within a couple of weeks, he was dropping by her house at the slightest excuse and his mother was leaving hints that she'd like to meet the new girl.

The copper room was rarely on his mind, until he got a call from Uncle Greg.

"Jereomy, do you think you could keep a eye on the house for a week or so. I need to make a presentation at a company in California."

"Sure. I'm in the neighborhood all the time anyway."

"So I've noticed. If I'd thought you and Lil were going to hit it off, I would have introduced you years ago."

"What are you presenting?"

"Not something I want to talk about over the phone, but I bet you can guess."

. . .

A couple of days later, Jerry picked up the keys to the house and drove his uncle down to Baldwin Field outside of Quincy. A copper box the size of a desktop printer was going with him. Greg spent part of the drive wrapping it carefully. He had to get it though the flight inspectors.

Greg nodded when he asked. "Yes, it's a little version. This is actually my first prototype. In my first experiments, I could turn a slice of bread moldy in seconds, but I had to have the big version so that I could prove to myself that it was happening as I hoped it was. See, there's a timer inside, since I can't control it from the outside. It's a little clumsy to use, but it works."

. . .

After school, Lil sent him a text message:
Prbly shouldn't see you tonight. Heavy study. I'll be up all night.

He texted back:
Gotta visit Uncles house anyway. Give me five minutes.

The idea had been hovering in the back of his head for some time, and if she needed study time, why not? Greg had agreed to let him continue using the copper room, he just hadn't needed it as much since he was spending much more time than usual with the books in Lil's house.

And it was study time for the most part. Lil's parents didn't hover, overtly. But the doorway between the dining room table where they chatted over books and the kitchen was never closed. He could always see someone making trips to the refrigerator. Her little sister Meg did come to spy, but Lil shooed her away.

...

When he arrived, he texted her:
Come over, bring study materials.
She showed up at the door, carrying a book.
"Is that all?" he asked.
"I told you I can't take the time. Not tonight."
"Well, come on then, I've got to show you this. It'll change everything."
He led her to the copper room. She eyed the bed with suspicion. He flushed. "Not what you're thinking. I study here all the time. It's very productive. This room can make time stand still."
She frowned.
"It's true. Uncle Greg is an inventor. This room is designed to make time flow at a different rate. I'll show you."
He led her to the door and had her take note of the time on the big clock outside. He then sealed the door, set the rate to 100X and started it.
She crossed her arms. "Now what?"
"We wait five minutes. You promised me that much, didn't you?"
While they waited, he talked about what he had done before and how the magic study sessions had gotten him ahead of the game. "It's a big secret. Industrial level. Greg is off to California right now to get buyers. But we can use it, at least until he gets back."
"Time is up," she said, looking at her phone.

Jerry opened the door and showed her the grandfather clock. Only seconds had passed. She was suspicious. "Try it with my cell phone." She set it outside and they waited another five minutes while she sat at the desk and tried to read.

"It's true!" she said when they opened the door and she picked up her phone. "You couldn't have faked the cell phone time."

"And that means we've only used a few seconds of your evening. Stay here to study and you can get it all done before supper."

"I'll need my other books. I didn't really understand what you wanted me to bring. Wait here."

She slipped back across the yard and returned with her satchel. "I *have* to be back home in ten minutes, or they'll notice I'm gone."

"No problem. How many hours do you need?"

"Ahh. Make it three."

"Okay." A hundred and eighty minutes. He set the rate dial to 2000X. "We'll be gone five seconds." He flipped the switch beside the dial.

. . .

There was only one chair at the table so he let her have it while he stretched out on the bed and bunched the pillows up into a back rest. He had his own studying to do, but he positioned himself so he could keep an eye on her.

A few minutes later, Lil asked, "Jerry? Are you sure this is real?"

"Absolutely. What could I possibly gain by pretending?"

She nodded, and went back to work. But an hour later, he had to reassure her again.

He had closed his eyes and had actually drifted off when she woke him.

"You snore."

He blinked his eyes. "Sorry. How long was I out? Besides, I don't snore."

She pulled out her full-featured cell phone and with an evil grin, played a recording of his noises.

"My phone says we've been here two and a half hours, but there's no signal."

"You wanted three, are you wanting to quit early?"

She nodded, with a twist of her mouth. "I know I'm probably okay. But if I were really three hours late getting home, you can't imagine the trouble I'd be in. They keep me on a short leash."

He grinned, "I don't blame them, with a daughter as pretty as you and all those horny teenage guys wanting to drag you off to bed."

He pulled her down on top of him.

She squealed, "You jerk." But she gave him a quick kiss before struggling back to her feet. "But really, I'm starved."

She packed her books. He waited until she was ready.

"Open your phone and watch the clock as I open the door." He turned off the time distortion and opened the heavy door. There was a little whoosh as the air inside and out equalized.

As they walked out of the copper room, she said, "Hey, signal and...the clock shifted back!"

"Right. Your phone just got corrected. Just five seconds, right?"

She nodded. "About, it doesn't show seconds."

He stopped at the doorway to coach her. "Remember, you just left your house. If they catch you, it was just to say 'Hi', or to give me a book or something."

She nodded and kissed him quickly before leaving. She started to run and then caught herself and slowed back to a walk.

...

Alone and packing up his own books, he could still feel the kiss and the ones that had come before. He had a feeling that she'd want more extended study sessions, and he took a closer look at the room. There were some things he could do to make it more comfortable for her, before next time.

...

"How is your studying going?" Jerry called as soon as he suspected she was out of school.

He could hear traffic noises over the phone. She was driving home. "I have a lot to get done tonight, and there's a video I'm supposed to watch on the computer at eight." It was a leading question, he was sure.

"Hmm. I can't help you with the video if it's live, but the study room is available."

"Great. Is it okay if I drop by at about 8:30?"

"No problem."

He patted the bundle he had in his Jeep. That would give him all the time he needed to get the rest of his alterations all set up.

...

Lil showed up in the darkened house. "Jerry?"

"Back here."

She carried her satchel into the copper room. "Wow."

He beamed. There was a second table with plates and a second chair. He had a mini-fridge plugged into the electrical system, with a microwave oven resting on top of it. "I have food that'll let us extend the study session for more than just a couple of hours. There's extension speakers for your music if you want. All the comforts of home."

"Crank it up. I've got a lot of work to do before class tomorrow."

With two thousand times as much time on their hands, it was a pleasant session. Lil worked her notes on the video she had watched at her house while it was still fresh in her mind. Jerry was working on a research paper for his advanced social studies course and had archived dozens of websites on his laptop during the day so that he could read them at his leisure. He had a stack of old history books that he'd been wanting to read for years, and this was the only place where he'd likely have the time to read them.

After an hour or so, they took a break and he re-heated some fried chicken in the microwave. They took a five minute real time break to use the bathroom and then sealed the room again for more study.

...

"My brain is fried." Jerry put down his book and stretched. "Care for a break? I've got twelve TV shows and a couple of movies on my laptop."

He nuked some popcorn and after a moment's testing the waters, they both stretched out on the bed with the laptop between them. Lil dozed off before the movie was half over. Jerry watched her breathe, and let it run. He intended to wake her when it was done, but he closed his eyes as well.

Neither of them noticed when the refrigerator when silent. Nor when the lights went dark nearly an hour later. When the air scrubber reached its low-voltage warning, it shut down and beeped an alert. The time distortion controls received a signal from the scrubber's shutdown and turned off the time circuitry. The muffled chime of the outside clock wasn't loud enough to wake either of them.

...

Lil dreamed she was suffocating. She was being chased and the walls were closing in on her. Her eyes opened to a room so totally dark that only the sleep indicator on the laptop gave any light.

"Jerry. Jerry! Wake up!" she shook him. Sluggishly, he opened his eyes.

"What? What's going on?"

"The lights are out. Did you turn the lights off?"

"Um. No." He slid out of bed and stumbled to the floor. He was panting. "I think the air's gone stale."

"Get us out of here!"

He nodded, although she couldn't see him. He kept one hand on the bed as he walked over to the table and flipped the switch on the lamp. It didn't work.

"Lil, see if your phone or my laptop can shine any light."

She lit up the laptop's screen, but it went dark again several seconds later. By the time she'd gotten her cell phone screen glowing brightly, he'd already reached the time controls and manually pushed the switch to the off position.

She walked over to join him as he unsealed the door and fresh air came in with a whoosh.

"Uh, oh."

"What?" she asked. He pointed at the big clock, barely visible in the dim, outside light, filtering in from the streetlights. "The time slowdown must have failed. It's nearly midnight."

"What!" She checked her cell phone and confirmed it. "I'm gonna be in so much trouble!"

She stumbled back into the copper room and collected her books by cell phone light.

They had barely stepped out the front door when her mother called out, "There you are young lady! Come home this instant."

Lil brushed at her hair, instantly aware that she probably looked like she'd just gotten out of bed. Jerry kept his distance. Lil's mother's look was one to peel paint at a distance. Her father came out on the porch. "Perhaps, it would be better if you left now."

Jerry nodded, "I'll just get my books."

He gathered up his stuff quickly. It was plain what had happened. His extra creature comforts like the refrigerator, microwave, laptop charger and music system had drained the limited battery supply. He found the charging cord and fished it out the metal doorway to an outside wall plug and hurriedly headed home.

His parents were up. They'd gotten a call from Lil's parents, trying to find her. They even asked if he and Lil were having sex. He denied it emphatically. They were just studying. He'd played a movie as they were taking a break and they both fell asleep. That was all.

His dad, who probably didn't believe that was the whole story, nodded and just said that it would probably be best if he stayed clear of Lil for a while. Her parents could be very protective of her.

...

In his room, he worried about how much trouble he was in. On his laptop, a chat message appeared. *Timegirl* wanted to be his friend.

Timegirl: I'm stuck for at least a month. They took my phone, and probably are going to check all my messages and email.

Lamentation: I got asked The Question and I'm not even sure they believed me.

Timegirl: What did you say?

Lamentation: We studied. We took a break to watch a movie on my laptop and we both dozed off.

Timegirl: About what I said. Meg took the opportunity to report that she'd seen me going back and forth to the neighbor's house. The little spy! My parents went to your uncle's house and knocked on the door, but it didn't wake us up, so they don't believe we were there.

Lamentation: Sturdy walls. Not loud enough to wake us up. Plus, my car was parked around the corner. They probably didn't see it.

Timegirl: So we're sunk. No special study sessions when I need them the most.

Lamentation: I'll still have to go by the house. Promised Greg. Discovered the problem. Ran out of battery juice. Working on a solution.

Timegirl: Don't flaunt it in front of my parents. Don't be visible. Don't make them angry.

Lamentation: Good idea. When are they gone?

Timegirl: Dad 8AM-6PM weekdays. Mom works noon to 9PM. Plus church hours.

Lamentation: Could I meet you at church?

Timegirl: Might be pushing it.

Lamentation: Internet it is, then. For now.

. . .

As a senior with lots of special activities, he could wrangle some special hours away from school. He took advantage of that to get the oxygen tanks refilled and made sure the microwave and the refrigerator were disconnected from the battery system. He made sure the refrigerator could only run from the charging side of the circuit. Maybe he could fill the freezer compartment with campers blue ice or something. The batteries charged back up with no problem and he traced the wiring to make sure he understood what changes Uncle Greg had added that he wasn't aware of. The safety switch that turned off the time circuits when the air started to go bad was perfectly sensible, but if he'd been more aware of it, maybe he wouldn't have allowed it to get that bad in the first place.

Greg's air system was designed to keep itself topped up as long as there was electricity to make it work. There was even a zeolite system that would pump up a tank with oxygen enriched air. The carbon dioxide system needed chemicals replaced from time to time, but there was a big canister of the stuff already available in his workshop. Other than that, all it needed was electricity. Unfortunately, it didn't recharge automatically. That extension cord fished out the open door was the only way to make it work.

. . .

Lamentation: System is fixed. Even added a LOUD alarm when battery is low. Problem shouldn't happen again.

Timegirl: Can't plan anything. They're watching me all the time now.

Lamentation: Sorry. I'll keep everything ready, in case you need it.

Timegirl: I wish. The Pom Squad tryouts are starting for the next class and I'm needed to help coach the younger ones. That plus finals is burying me.

Lamentation: I'll help with the cheerleaders ;)

Timegirl: Don't you dare.

. . .

Jerry, with the time expansion at his fingertips, was on top of every assignment—so much so that he was finding real time going by much too slowly. He resorted to doing all his study time in the copper room, with his car stashed in the Saints Avenue Cafe parking lot a couple of blocks away. He had a walking route that stayed out of sight of the main traffic and entered his uncle's house from the rear, never in sight of Lil's house. He avoided turning on the lights and made sure he wasn't making any noise noticeable to the neighbors. But when he went home, with nothing but TV and sleep to occupy him, he was depressed.

His parents noticed. His mother asked how he was doing. His father quizzed him about how his school work was holding up. "Don't worry," was his answer to everything.

When Greg called to check up on him, he said everything was going fine. The demo in California had gone off well, but there were extensive negotiations. Everything was taking longer than he had expected.

"Take your time," Jerry said.

"Easy for you to say. I'm stuck in real time."

...

Sunday, he slipped out early. His parents didn't make a point of going to church, and even when they did, it was in Lewistown where they lived, not down the road at her church in Canton, so he hoped to be gone and back before they noticed.

Lil was a choir member, and he knew she'd never miss it. He sat in the back, well away from where she or her family sat. He came in late and planned to leave early.

She noticed. Not that she gave any sign, other than her smile, but she was in particularly strong voice that morning. Jerry slipped away before the final prayer, and thought he'd gotten away with it.

...

Timegirl: I saw you.

Lamentation: You were great.

Timegirl: Unfortunately, I wasn't the only one.

Lamentation: Oh?

Timegirl: Yep. Remember the Robinsons? They met you during the Easter presentation. They saw you and asked my parents about you.

Lamentation: Oops. Problems?

Timegirl: Maybe. Parents can't gripe about you being at church. Not seemly. But they gave me the lecture again. No dating through the end of the semester. And of course, they're planning to ship me off to summer camp nearly immediately after that.

Lamentation: What kind of 'camp'?

Timegirl: Oh, it's okay. I signed up for it on my own. Church camp, Been there every year since I was 11. I was planning to be a senior counselor this year. I just didn't plan on meeting you.

Lamentation: How do you go to this place?

Timegirl: Too late for you. It's popular and they fill up half year in advance. No chance we'll get back together until at least mid-July.

Lamentation: *No* chance? What if I left the back door unlocked?

Timegirl: Don't get your hopes up.

...

That night, before Lil's family was back from Sunday evening service, Jerry loaded his computer with several website archives and locked himself into the copper room for some planning.

While his parents didn't bother him with questions about where he'd been and what he'd been doing, it was different with Lil and she'd need all the help she could get.

After a couple of days, her parents had given her phone back, but they were still likely to monitor her texting at any time, so it made sense to stick to this other messaging system that they weren't likely to tap. He couldn't count on her seeing his notices quickly, so if he came up with a plan, he'd need to notify her well in advance.

Jerry had read enough history books to know that complex battle plans hardly ever worked out in real life, Clausewitz and a half-dozen other generals made a point of it, so he had little hope that his schemes could actually work. But he had to try something!

Her car was sitting idle while she was grounded. Her mother took her to school and her father picked her up afterwards, unless there were some event that kept her late. And then she would call and be picked up by one or the other.

It wasn't likely he could pick her up at school and not have the word get back to her parents. But what if her parents couldn't pick her up? What then?

All Lil needed was fifteen minutes home alone. That would be long enough to bring her books over, spend a whole day together to study and talk and just be together, and then get her back home with nothing to make her folks worried.

So, how to put her parents out of the picture for a few minutes?

Difficult, since they could potentially back each other up if they had car trouble. Including Lil's car, they had three. But that could be changed.

He slipped into the Lil's yard and made a couple of tiny changes. He loosened the engine control computer connector on her car, and with a valve stem wrench, unscrewed the valve in her father's driver side front tire until there was just a slight hiss of escaping air. No real damage, but if things went well...

Jerry slipped back to the house unseen. He called home and told his parents he'd be studying all night at Uncle Greg's house. His mother grumbled, but didn't object too much.

Now to wait. Or maybe not!

He went into the copper room and checked the 'dangerous' time acceleration controls. He'd avoided them like the plague, but Greg's explanations had been clear enough. He adjusted the dial. 60X, the slowest, was too slow. 3600X acceleration would give him one hour per second. Good enough. He counted seven seconds.

...

Outside it was just dawn. Jerry nodded. It had worked.

Careful to avoid any lights, he moved to Greg's laundry room, where he could watch the driveway out the tiny window while he remained in the dark.

One tire was flat. So that had worked out.

After nearly twenty minutes, Mr. Nyson came out and quickly discovered his tire. He pulled out a little cigarette lighter air pump and refilled it, but by then, Mrs. Nyson and Lil had already headed off to school. No one even thought to check Lil's car. Soon everyone was gone.

Jerry packed his own school things and walked over to his Jeep. The second act would play out after school, and it all depended on whether Mr. Nyson got his tire fixed or not.

...

Lamentation: When do you get out of school today?

Timegirl: Late, because of cheerleader tryouts. Why do you ask?

Lamentation: The study room is lonely for you. If you get a chance, dash over, the back door will be open.

Timegirl: Not likely. Dad will pick me up and send me straight to my room. They're on to you. Lurking in the house next door.

Lamentation: He drives you home every day?

Timegirl: Lately. Before our oops, sometimes Shelia would drop me off, but not now.

...

Jerry was waiting, after school. His heart went tripping when a strange car drove up and Lil hopped out, dressed in her cheerleader outfit, with her school bags. She waved to her friend and then walked towards her house. Just as the car drove out of sight, she made a dash towards the gap in the back hedge.

"Jerry? Are you there?"

"Just waiting for you." She dashed into the copper room and he began closing the door.

She beamed at him, setting down her bags. "You planned this, didn't you?"

He nodded. "I'm surprised it actually worked."

"You're a genius." She jumped up into his arms.

He wasn't braced and barely caught her, bumping up against the wall and then falling down on one knee.

"Oops. Sorry." she smiled. He kissed her.

"I guess I'd better start the time switch..."

She looked up. "What's that noise?"

"I don't know." There was a tone, like a ragged high note being played softly on a flute.

He stood up and checked the dial.

The wrong switch was thrown. In a panic, he slapped at it. The tone went away.

Lil saw the look on his face. "What's wrong?"

His mind was in a whirl. What had really happened?

"The time accelerator got switched on when I fell against it."

"What does that mean?"

He pulled the locking bolt on the door. "It means we jumped ahead in time."

She put her hand to her mouth. "How much? If they think ..."

He opened the door and a swirl of dust showed in an instant that something was very wrong.

Year 153

They stepped out into the hallway. The old clock was gone. Some of the wallboard was broken, showing the bones of the house as if someone had come in with sledgehammers and trashed the place. Jerry went straight to the front door, Lil following closely behind. The door hinges were stiff when he pushed it open. The only thing visible was a high stone fence circling the property. It seemed even taller than the house.

Lil was shaking. "I need to go home." She was holding her cell phone. There was no signal.

He nodded. They would be in big trouble, no matter what, but that couldn't be helped.

"I think...I think we went more than a few hours."

Lil was eyeing the large sprawling oak tree that over-shaded the stone fence. It hadn't been there in the yard before.

To the right was a doorway in the stone wall, eight feet high, with a solid iron gate embedded in it. He tugged at the latch, but it was frozen. Rust marked his hand. "I can't get it open."

"We're trapped?"

"Let's keep looking."

They circled the house. The iron gate was the only exit. "Let's see if there are some tools."

Lil was looking down at the ground.

"What is it?" he asked.

"The wall goes past the old hedge." She kicked at the dirt. "This is part of my driveway."

They both were seeing the same things, but neither wanted to say it out loud. A lot of time had passed.

She turned and grabbed hold of him. Her shaking had become uncontrollable. "Jerry! What have I done?"

They sat on the steps. "You didn't do anything. I'm the one who got you into this."

"But I knocked you against the controls..."

"Stop it. Let's find out what happened."

He didn't want to let go of her. He was as spooked as she was. If they were really in the future, everything they knew, all the rules, everything they'd planned...all were out the window.

He didn't even know what to do first.

Lil was shaking and it occurred to him that it wasn't just shock. The air was cold. He looked up at the big tree and it was plain as day that half the leaves were gone.

"Lil. It's autumn. It's cold out. Let's get back inside. No matter what. We can't afford to get sick."

She sniffed and nodded. Inside, they looked around the other rooms of the house. It had been ransacked long ago. Closets were emptied, drawers were spilled out on the ground. There were some rotted fabrics, old towels and draperies.

But no tools.

They went back into the copper room and closed the door. She picked up her bag.

"Could you turn your back. I want to change clothes."

"I can go outside."

"No! Don't. I don't want you out of my sight."

He faced the wall and shortly she was in a longer skirt and packed away her cheerleader suit.

"How far into the future are we?"

Jerry shrugged. "Decades, at least. The house is neglected, but not ancient. The tree is at least 50 years old." He got up and carefully looked at the control dial. "This was pushed well past the calibrated portion. How long were we moving? Twenty seconds?"

"About that. I wasn't paying attention." She shook her head.

"I wish there was something in the house, a calendar or something."

"We need to see what's outside the wall."

He nodded. "I need to find a way to force that lock. I wish there was a crowbar or something."

"I could climb the tree."

He looked at her skeptically. "Are you sure?"

She nodded. "Just give me a boost to the low branch and I can get the rest of the way up. It would at least give us a view of what's outside."

He insisted she wear his jacket, and braced his back against the tree, letting her climb him. She was a cheerleader and as short as she was, she was often on the top tier of the pyramids. "But no looking up my skirt!"

He just grunted and said nothing.

"I'm up." She moved quickly through the branches until she was above the level of the wall.

"What do you see?"

She said nothing and moved even higher. Jerry followed her position, just to be in place, should she fall.

"Lil?"

"I'm trying to make sense of it all."

"Just tell me what you see."

"Okay. Almost all the houses are gone. My house...is gone, but I can see the foundation. There are trees everywhere, but it's a mix. Probably it's everybody's landscaping trees grown old."

"So the town is deserted?"

"Not completely. Off towards the river, I can see buildings. But they're strange."

"How strange?"

She turned and looked in another direction. "Jerry. There are animals."

"What kind?"

"I can't make them out. They're small. A flock of rabbits maybe. Hundreds of them."

"Maybe you should come back down."

"Okay." She started reversing her route through the limbs, taking her time.

"Jerry! I see an airplane." She pointed.

He had to move to make it out through the branches. It looked small, or else very high. It made no noise and it was quickly gone.

He moved back to Lil's position. When she reached the bottom branch, she smiled. "Catch me?"

He held out his arms and she dropped right into them.

"Whoo. I'm not used to this cheerleader stuff."

"You did okay. But let's go back inside. I'm cold."

...

"Can you describe the buildings you saw?"

"Better than that. I had my phone. I took pictures."

Jerry closed the door behind them, once they turned the lights back on. It just felt safer.

Once Lil flipped past some cheerleader pictures, there was a shot over the trees. Two large structures were visible near where the old fuel storage tanks had been. They were streamlined and huge, like enormous cruise liners, but with no deck. It was windows all the way up.

"Those have to be at the shore. Maybe in the river."

But with the exception of a few down town buildings, their whole city was overgrown. It was turning back into a forest. Maybe there were still some houses in use, but at least the closer neighborhood was all deserted.

...

"Jerry, if this is like a time machine," she asked, carefully considering her words, "which took us to the future, is there a way to put it into reverse, and take us back?"

He didn't answer, not for several minutes. He didn't want to lie to her.

"Uncle Greg only talked about changing the rate of time. He could slow it down or speed it up. He never even hinted at making it go in reverse. And I don't know anything about how it works. Nothing about the science. I know the room is copper because it has to be electrically sealed, but that's about it. It takes some electricity to run, but..."

He paused, with a deep frown as he stared at the floor.

"But what?" She searched his face for any hint of what he was thinking. Was it another disaster?

He looked at her. "It requires electricity. All our electricity comes from those batteries. In two days of careful use, they'll be drained and we won't have use of the tools or the lights, no way to recharge our computers, and certainly no way to run the time circuits. I recharged the batteries by running an extension cord out the door and plugging it into the wall. But I'd be shocked if the outlets are still active. If we're going to use the time shifter again, we'll need to do so quickly, before we're stranded in this year."

She tugged the cover off the bed and wrapped it around her shoulder. "It's getting cold, too. We probably don't have heat either."

He remembered a few fallen branches. "We could probably start a fire. Hmm. Maybe I could start a fire, but is that even a good idea? Should we advertise our presence? What do you think?"

She grumbled. "Why didn't we land in summer?"

"That's an idea! We landed here randomly. Why not shift another six months and skip the cold weather? I'm not in love with the idea of risking snow when we don't have a way to stay warm."

She looked over at the controls on the wall. "We just did twenty seconds and lost years? Do we have enough control to pick a season?"

He peered at the dial. "Uncle Greg had calibrated four settings. 60X, which is one second gives you a minute, 3600X, or one second equals one hour. I used that successfully this morning. The next one is 80,000X, which is a little less than one second per day, and 250,000X which works out to...seventy hours per second. He never calibrated beyond that. And the setting we were at is way over here at the mid range of the dial, and that looks like decades per second."

He dug out his phone and pulled up the calculator app. "So... if we wanted to go six months into the future, we could...that's sixty-two seconds at the 250,000X mark. What do you think?"

She stared at the dial with a pouty expression. "Do it. But mark the setting we used to get here, just in case we find a way to reverse it."

"Good idea." He pulled out a pen and added a line at the spot. He really didn't believe they had a chance at all to reverse time, but it was better to stay positive.

Carefully, he lined the dial up to 250,000X. "Ready."

She took a deep breath and nodded. "Do it."

Click.

"Is it working?"

Jerry nodded, watching seconds pass by on the stopwatch app on his cell phone. "It appears to be."

"It's not making that noise."

"Maybe it only happens when you're moving through time faster."

The phone's countdown counter clicked to zero, and he flipped the switch off.

"I'm going to check." He unsealed the door. This time there was a slight whiff of air as the pressure equalized.

Year 154

She set the blanket aside and followed. It was dark outside.

Neither of them had flashlights, but cell phones worked.

Outside the front door, a balmy spring breeze confirmed their time shift.

He muttered, "Wow, look at that sky."

The stars were brilliant. There was no sky glow other than in the direction of downtown.

Lil pointed, "Look at the satellites!"

There were dozens of moving dots in the star field. After a moment, one brighter than Venus passed by overhead.

"It's a space age."

Jerry said nothing. Maybe it *was* a space age. Or maybe those were just abandoned relics of a different time. He couldn't quite reconcile the abandoned city with what he saw above.

"Well, we won't freeze tonight. And since my body clock says it's night time as well, I need to grab a quick supper snack and get some rest. My brain is running on empty."

She took his hand. "Did you say food?"

...

He had planned for twenty four hours, with sandwich makings and cokes in the refrigerator.

"Shut the door quickly to keep the cool in. It's not plugged in any more. We need to limit the electricity to one overhead light."

Lil fixed the sandwiches, conscious that food that couldn't be refrigerated didn't need to be hoarded.

Jerry took his coke and sandwich and said, "Let's eat on the porch. Save the light."

They sat and watched the lights overhead as they ate.

"What do we do tomorrow?"

He shrugged. "Try to get outside this stone wall. There are all kinds of answers out there if we could get down to the town."

She leaned against him in the dark. "I need to find out what year it is. If there's any chance my family is still alive..."

"I know."

He put his arm around her. "When it's light out, I want to search the house again, from top to bottom. I keep thinking Uncle Greg would have left me a message. He would have understood what happened when he got back from his trip and found the copper room sealed tight and invulnerable. He'd try to contact me. I know he would!"

"What do you mean invulnerable?"

"Nobody outside could open the door. It didn't happen, not over decades of time. And you know they tried. Since time was frozen inside, no tool would be able to dislodge any molecules caught in the time effect."

"So we're safe inside the room?"

"Yes, but we'd be blazing across the years again. It's hardly something we'd want to do just to lock the door at night."

"What about the other way, like when we stopped time to study?"

"Then we'd be safe because the outside would be frozen. If a hoard of zombies wanted to attack, they'd be frozen. But it wouldn't help, because sooner or later, we'd run out of air or electricity."

She nodded. "Got it." She yawned. "Only travel to the future to escape the zombies."

"Let's get you to bed."

She perked up. "What do you mean by that buster?"

"What I said. Now let's make sure we pick up the scraps. Let's not attract ants or hoards of rabbits."

They went back inside and he sealed the door.

"Do we take shifts or do you feel safe enough inside a locked metal room inside a house inside a high stone wall?"

She picked up the blanket and began making the bed. "I don't feel safe. I probably won't ever feel safe. But we both need sleep."

He checked the electrical system. Then shook his head. "I'm not thinking straight. We can't leave the door locked. The air system would run the battery down too soon. Do you understand?"

She nodded. He unsealed the door and left it open a foot.

She kicked off her shoes and slipped under the covers. "You can share the bed."

He sighed. "This wasn't how I planned it."

"Planned what?"

"A twenty four hour getaway from school pressure and unreasonable parents. Time to catch up on your studies and time to get to know you better. And in the best of all possible worlds, maybe some make-out time on this bed."

"Not tonight."

"I know." He turned off the last light and moved by feel to the bed. He kicked off his shoes as well and slid under the covers with her. "Maybe not ever."

"Not ever?"

"Who knows? The instant I took you away from your parents, the rules changed. You were protected. Kept safe from guys like me. Now you're not. So I have to be your protector."

"And if I don't want to be protected?"

He put his arm behind her pillow. "That would be nice to think about. But only when we're safe."

She snuggled close, her face against his shirt. "Safe is nice."

He stayed motionless in the dark, listening as she drifted off to sleep. Painfully aware of the feel of her, he was close enough to be conscious of her warmth. But it was all true. He got her into this. He was responsible for her safety. And she had to be kept safe from more than just zombies, ants and rabbits. He hadn't really planned on sleeping with her, so he hadn't stocked up on condoms. If she were on contraceptives, likely she would run out soon. Maybe this future they were stranded in had good medical care and maybe it didn't. One of Lil's biggest hazards right now was him.

...

"Jerry."

He blinked, and was disoriented. There was daylight coming through the door. Lil was a silhouette in the light. "Hmm. Yes?"

"The toilet outside doesn't flush."

He struggled to shake off a nightmare about zombies. "We have a chemical toilet we can use for emergencies, but with no water in the house pipes, that means I have to find a way to open the iron gate in the stone wall. We only have a few cokes, and we'll need an outside supply of water before they run out."

He made use of the un-flushable bathroom toilet himself, and then made sure the door was closed tightly. It would get ripe soon enough.

She grumbled, "Well, high on my priority list is shampoo. There wasn't even an old bar of soap in the bathroom. When we get enough water, I'm claiming enough for a good bath. I'm going to complain..."

She stopped mid-sentence. He saw tears welling up.

"Save your complaints for later. Right now I need to start my house search."

She shook her head. "I wasn't going to complain to you." She sniffed. "I was going to complain to Coach Henson. For not letting me take time to shower after cheerleader tryouts."

"Well, I've got plenty of complaints myself. I guess they all got lucky. They missed out on our righteous anger."

"Yeah." She agreed quietly.

"Well, let's open every drawer, and check every cabinet. Start in the kitchen." He didn't know what they were looking for, but anything could be useful, especially any tools.

...

Thirty minutes later, Jerry located an attic access-hatch in the ceiling of a closet.

"Lil! Get up here."

She scrambled up beside him in the dark attic. The glow of his cell phone illuminated a switch panel with a scrawled message:

> "Jereomy, I forgot to mention in the manual, you'll have to remove the covers from the roof solar panels. Here's hoping they're still functional when you need them.—Greg Montain 2051"

"Oh!" Her exclamation was a cry of despair.

"What's wrong?" He was overjoyed. There might be a solution to their power problem. And Uncle Greg had understood what had happened to them and made provisions to help.

"If he wrote this in 2051," she rubbed the old corroded markings, "then there's no chance my family is still alive."

He put his arm around her shoulder. "I know. I've suspected it, because this place is so neglected. In 2051, Uncle Greg, and my parents, would have been in their eighties. I'm sure Greg bought out the neighboring houses when the area was abandoned and put up the stone wall around this place for our protection."

She put her feelings away and helped him get through the access port at the south end of the peaked roof. Working without a net to crawl from the attic to the roof was nerve-wracking, but he managed to discover the latches that secured the protective covers over the solar panels. One by one, he slid the covers back to expose the black surface to daylight. They weren't like any solar panel design he'd ever seen. He walked carefully, but the one time he put his weight in the wrong place, the panel didn't crack. He held his breath until he stepped back on the ridges. If the system worked, great, but until they managed to break free of their prison, repairs were impossible.

...

"Cross your fingers." He flipped the switches and indicator lights lit up, showing 60% capacity.

Down stairs, he reached for a wall switch. The ceiling light slowly ramped up to full brightness.

"We have power. We have power!"

Rushing as if it would vanish in seconds, he hurriedly dug out the charging cable from the copper room and plugged it in. The light dimmed slightly.

"Okay, we have limited power. But it should be enough to keep the room charged up."

He could see Lil was pleased that he was pleased, but she didn't fully understand.

He explained his feelings. "With full power, we can sleep with the door closed, and we can escape to another time if this one proves dangerous."

"Good." Just then there was a sound from the bathroom. Cautiously, they checked. Rusty water was splashing from the faucet.

"Do you think Uncle Greg put a well on this property? We might just have water."

He checked and the toilet tank had filled. He disposed of the mornings activities. It began filling again.

Lil was bent over the sink. "The water is getting clearer. Thank you Jerry's Uncle Greg!" She pushed him out of the bathroom with one hand while unbuttoning her blouse with the other. "Get out. I'm taking a bath while I have the chance."

...

It was clear there were parts of the house, like some kind of well and water pump, that were hidden, even from his first two searches. But now he had something to work with. The switch panel in the attic took in wires from the solar cells on the roof and distributed the juice throughout the house. One of those switches probably controlled the water pump.

He pulled out a ring-bound notebook from his school supplies and went up into the attic to trace the connections.

...

Lil peeked out the bathroom door. There was noise from the kitchen. She dashed to the open door of the copper room and raced back holding her gym bag and locked the bathroom door behind her. Ten minutes later she came out dressed in tee shirt and gym shorts with her other clothes dripping from the shower curtain rod. She brushed at her hair as she went hunting for Jerry.

He was still in the kitchen, halfway inside the barren pantry.

"What are you up to?"

He backed out. "I just found the water system. It's like nothing I've ever seen. I was expecting to find a pump, and I was worried...I mean a decades-old water pump, right? I wanted to make sure it wasn't in need of lubrication or something. But this thing is solid state. No moving parts. I can't understand how it works."

She knelt down beside him and looked into the pantry, where there was an access panel in the back. "You mean it's like something futuristic or something?"

"Don't laugh at me. Yes. That's what I mean. I was just trying to be careful."

"Well, be careful and make sure you don't break it. I've only got the clothes I brought with me and I'll need to keep them washed."

...

They sat on the porch, eating sandwiches and enjoying the gently swaying branches of the tree and the thick, if ragged, carpet of grass in the yard. This season of the year, the outlines of the old driveway were much more clearly defined. Jerry was thinking about the driveway his folks had put in when he was ten. The work crew and laid down a gridwork of rebar iron and stones before pouring the concrete over it. If this one was done the same way, breaking up some of the old eroded concrete might expose some of those iron bars, and they might make the tools he'd need to force open the stone wall gate.

He had to get out. Their food would run out in a day or so. At worst, Lil had seen rabbits. He could hunt, even if it was just throwing rocks or building snares.

He had to plan for the future. One of those futures was living in this house with the minimal amenities Uncle Greg had left them, hunting for food, maybe with a garden. Living here with Lil wouldn't be a bad life. It wasn't what they'd planned just yesterday, but was an option. It was still too soon to discuss it with her. He couldn't just claim her.

"I'm surprised," she said, "that I'm not a total basket case. I mean... lost in time. My family is probably dead, even."

"It's not real," he agreed. "There wasn't the chaos of a car wreck, or a gunshot, or serious-faced doctor in a hospital waiting room. With us, it was just a little noise in the air, and suddenly our lives changed. Maybe it takes some trauma to shake up the neurons. I guess I'd half expect Uncle Greg to materialize in a time machine and take us back home. I hope when my nervous breakdown happens, we'll at least be somewhere safe. Somewhere I can recover."

She began to add something, when there came a banging noise on the outside iron gate.

...

They both froze. Jerry hopped to his feet and waved Lil to stay back out of sight. He walked up to the gate. There was no gap around the edge, but there was a shadow of someone's feet just visible in the tiny bottom gap.

"Hello," he yelled. "Who is that?"

"Park Regat here. This is a restricted area. Open up."

"Uh. Sorry. I didn't know that. Why is it restricted?" He was just winging it. The man sounded like a policeman. What was a 'Regat'?

"Don't joke. This is Henderson Mutagenic Reserve."

"Wow. Is that bad?"

"Yes. Now open up and I'll arrange a drop to come pick you up."

Jerry didn't know what to do. He didn't want the local cops coming down on him, but the only control he had—his only hope for safety, was to stay with the copper room.

He shook the lock on the iron door. "I'm sorry, but I think this old lock is frozen solid. You don't have a key on you do you?"

It shook from the other side. "How did you get in there? The Eye Spy showed the roof changing color. What's going on?"

"Oh, sorry. I just turned on the power system. Solar cells on the roof. Is that a problem? I can put it back."

"How did you get in?"

"I climbed the wall. But it's okay. I have my own transportation. You don't need to pick me up."

"Who are you? Some Circ?"

"Something like that. I assume I am safe here inside?"

"Probably, unless the army rats take it into their pea brains to tunnel under the wall. I'll be glad when we eradicate the last of them."

Jerry almost relayed the report Lil gave of seeing hundreds from the tree, but then he realized that was six months earlier.

"Um, Mr. Regat sir, I realize I dropped into this place without doing my homework. But seriously, my transportation will be back shortly and I'll be out of your hair. Is there anything I need to be aware of? Precautions to take?"

"You Circs are a pain. If I had a lifter or a grappling rope with me, I'd just take you with me, but I'll have to leave you here for today. If you're still in my loop three days from now, it'll be a different story. Heads up!"

The man tossed something over the wall. Jerry wasn't in position to catch it. The little tablet bounced, but showed no damage. He picked it up and the screen flickered as a place on the form filled in with an image of his face.

"Speak your name," said the gadget.

"Jeromy Harris." It appeared on the form, even spelled correctly. The software even made an estimate of this birthday—horribly wrong, but it couldn't have known about his time traveling.

"Profession?"

"Circ?" it was as good a guess as anything. The form filled in with, "Student/Circumnavigation/Historical" and a new field appeared, guessing that he was born on Ceres.

The asteroid?

"ID number?" He whispered his social security number. It took it, but added a three digit suffix.

The rest of the form appeared to be something like a traffic ticket. The violation was unauthorized camping in a restricted area. The penalty was 540°.

"Hey, do I just throw this thing back to you?"

"Yes."

He tossed it blindly.

The Park Regat said, "You'll have to take care of this before you leave Earth. Now like I said, I'll be swinging back through here in three days. Be gone by then. Remember that this is a mutagenic zone. You should not eat any flesh of any of the flagged new species. Just to be safe, you shouldn't eat anything you didn't bring in with you. Here's something for you to read." He pushed a pamplet under the gate. It barely slipped through.

"Ah. I'm not from around here. What does that stuff do to you?"

"Kids! Don't they give you any education before turning you loose on your historical tours? There are thirty-seven mutagenic zones on the planet. Speciation is accelerated here. Until the bad genes get weeded out, transcription codes can hop from animal to animal, making new varieties all the time. It's all explained in the text."

"Wow, that sounds like a problem. Will it ever stop?"

"Oh sure, in about a hundred years or so. That's what they tell me. Of course they said we'd have the army rats wiped out ten years ago, and their numbers are growing, if you can believe that. Anything else? I've got rounds to make."

"Ah. Do you have any extra snacks? My stuff is getting monotonous."

With a snort of disgust, he said, "Yes, heads up. And three days! I won't be so nice next time, no matter how rich your parents are."

The packed of food sailed over the wall and landed a couple of feet away.

"Thanks a lot. I appreciate it."

There was a whooshing sound and the Park Regat was gone.

Jerry picked up the food package and the pamphlet and looked around. "Lil?"

Up above, hiding behind a large tree branch, she replied, "Come help me down." She had brought out a chair and gotten herself up into the tree.

He helped her down. She held up her phone. "I got his picture." She showed it. A view looking down on a man in a brown uniform, features obscured by a helmet, riding some vehicle like a stretched 4-wheeler.

"Did you follow what we said?"

"Yes, you guys were yelling."

"We're in trouble."

"Afraid of a ticket?"

"Afraid that we could lose our ability to find a better time. We can't stay here."

She nodded seriously. "This mutagenic stuff scares me. I want kids, some day. Kids that look like me and their father. Not kids with fur and tails. You don't think we've already been contaminated, do you?"

"It didn't sound like it. What scares me is that I was already planning to go hunting, to add to our food supplies. I'd have never known." He stared at the pamphlet. It looked like it was made of plastic.

"It's not our time."

"No it's not."

...

Lil held up the food wrapping. "Packed in Chicago, 2163. I guess that settles it. We came about 150 years in twenty seconds."

"That matches what the ticket computer said. It guessed I was born May 2145, on Ceres."

"Space colonization," she said. "And rich kids from the colonies come to Earth as part of their education."

"It sounds like an exciting time. Do we stay or move on?"

She leaned against him. "I don't know. We've got a little time to decide, don't we?"

"Yes. Three days, he said. Maybe less than that if their computers don't like my personal information."

She pulled back, wrinkled her nose and frowned at him. "First order of business is to get your clothes washed. Is this all you've got?"

"Yes. This and my letter jacket. I didn't plan this."

"I guess I'm lucky I brought my gym clothes home. I've at least got something to change into. It'll have to do. We don't have any soap, but you can at least rinse out the stink. Go to the bathroom, wash your clothes and take a bath. Whether we have to jump to another era, or not, we should at least be clean."

"I'm not going to walk around naked."

She looked him up and down, fighting a grin. "My towel is big and it should be dry by now. Use it and your letter jacket until the rest of it dries out."

...

He did as he was told, although the terry cloth was hardly his favorite fabric, especially rinsed in hard water and dried without a fabric softener. It also limited what he could do without his kilt becoming untucked.

Lil enjoyed it, making comments about his hairy legs and the dimples on his knees. He wished she wouldn't tease him like that. With all her underwear and regular clothes still drying on the pole, and looking very cute in her minimal gym outfit, his thoughts kept returning to dangerous speculations.

Pulling himself back on track, he pulled out the pamphlet from the Park Regat and read about the rash of industrial accidents, terrorist and military actions that let the mutagenic plague loose in parts of the world. The pamphlet claimed the technology had been tamed, and all affected organisms could be treated to deactivate the susceptibility to accelerated mutation, but there were still patches of ground where native wildlife carried the taint, and short of nuking the ground to glass, they were just going to let the carriers die out. Since so many of the mutations were harmful, each generation had fewer and fewer contaminated members. Like the Regat said, in a hundred years, it would be totally under control. The contaminated areas were fenced off and evacuated of all residents. No one was supposed to go in without a permit.

"This area is like a genetic Chernobyl. They moved every one out and let it go back to nature."

Lil sat beside him on the bed. "Do you think they had contaminated people?"

"I'd bet on it. This mentions that terrorists and soldiers used it as a weapon. Probably lots of deformed babies, and then some viable ones with 'differences'. I bet if we choose to stay in this year, we'll find out pretty soon."

She snuggled closer. "I can understand accidents. Technology getting out of control. I can't understand people using it as a weapon."

"Unfortunately, I can."

She looked at him with a frown.

He shrugged. "Remember the story of Alfred Nobel? He made dynamite thinking that it was an explosive so dangerous that people wouldn't fight any more. That didn't work out like he thought. Then there was the atomic bomb, and from the way this pamphlet talks, people use those now, from time to time. Back in the Cold War, I was reading about the government policy of Mutually Assured Destruction and doomsday plans.

"I really don't think there's any weapon so horrible that someone won't eventually try to use it. If people would make serious plans to wipe out all life on the planet, it's not much of a stretch to imagine threatening to deform the babies of your enemies."

"You wouldn't do anything like that."

"No. Probably not. I can't imagine doing it. But I've got several history books in my backpack that prove that people can do the unthinkable when they are at war."

She hugged him tightly. "Jerry, if you don't mind. I don't want to stay here."

"Stay here in the house, or stay here in this year?"

"It says the mutagenics will be gone in a hundred years?"

"So it says."

"Then I think we should skip ahead two hundred. I had hopes that I might connect with my family. Maybe Meg, or her kids. But that's unlikely isn't it?"

"Considering that our home town was destroyed and that maybe everyone we knew, and all their kids and grandkids for several generations are now scattered, yes, I think it's unlikely. We're pretty much on our own."

"Do you think the house will still be here in 200 years?"

"I don't know. The copper room will, but the rest is subject to decay. We could lose our water supply and our electricity."

"We lose those anyway."

"Yeah."

They were silent in their gloom. After a while, as the outside began to get darker, Jerry asked, "Do you think my clothes are dry? I'm not going to sleep in a towel."

"We'll check in a minute." She began unsnapping the fasteners on his jacket.

"What are you doing?"

"I'm pretending. For just a little bit, I'm pretending I'm making out with my boyfriend, hiding out from my parents next door, just getting a little sweetness before I have to go back to my studies."

He kissed her. Pretend. It was unbearable sweetness, but he had to hold the line. He was her protector.

Too quickly, he had to stop. He whispered the word.

"Just another..."

He pulled her hand from under his jacket and kissed it. "We'll pretend again, soon." He slid out of the bed and had to keep a grip on the towel.

"Promise," she called after him as he hurried out the door.

His clothes were nearly dry. Enough so he could dress and take a couple of laps around the house to cool his blood down. Lil was everything he wanted, and he wanted her badly.

But he wanted her safe, and that was far from certain just yet. Maybe she didn't even realize what effect she had on him. They hadn't talked out that part of their relationship.

By the time stars and satellites were making their appearance, he wandered back in. Lil had pulled all her clothes off the shower rod and had dressed in her frilly blouse and dark skirt. Music was playing softly from her laptop.

"Jerry. There you are. I was wondering...I mean we hadn't actually agreed on what we're doing."

He nodded. "Head for the future. I don't have any strong attachment to now. Of course, there's no guarantee that we'll be in any better shape two hundred years from now, but I can risk it.

"But for now, I want to get a good nights sleep. Before we leave, I want to secure the water and electrical system, just in case."

She turned off her laptop and slipped under the covers. He turned off all the lights and propped the door open again. The batteries were nearly charged, but with the darkness, the house electricity shut down, and he didn't want to drain them by running the air system. Trying not to be obvious about it, he determined that Lil was under the sheet, so he slept on top of it. He held her hand, and tried not to think about anything else.

...

The noise woke him. Her presence was an overriding background. He couldn't help but be aware of her.

But her soft breathing was not what had woken him. It was the scratching.

The tree? Its wide branches shaded part of the roof. Was the wind blowing them?

It was dark, and he could either think of Lil just inches away, or the noise. He decided to get up and investigate. Outside, in the hallway, he could hear it even louder. At the front door it was clear. Something was scratching at the iron gate. Timidly, walking under the stars and the half-moon, he approached. The scratching, as if by hundreds of fingernails all at once, increased. They could hear him.

The moonlight wasn't enough to tempt him to climb the tree, like Lil had done, but he needed to know what was out there. He got closer and said, "Scat!"

There was a pause, and then the scratching began again, even more furiously. He got down on his knees and lowered his head, trying to peer through that tiny gap at the bottom. He couldn't see, but there was another noise, tiny, tiny voices. Rat voices.

Army rats. These were the vermin the Park Regat complained about. They had discovered their presence. What had he done wrong? Their noise? The water? Their picnic crumbs on the front porch?

Whatever it was, the rats were on his scent.

"Scat! Go away." He hammered on the gate with his fist. They didn't seem offended.

What had the Regat said? That the rats might take it into their heads to tunnel under the wall.

He got to his feet and dashed back into the house.

"Lil!" He shook her awake. Wide eyed and half asleep, she held the blanket to her chin.

"Lil, get up. The army rats are here. We're going to have to jump times immediately. Grab everything you left outside. Anything outside the copper room gets abandoned."

She slipped on her shoes and made a dash for the bathroom.

He weighed the risk of climbing into the attic and shutting down the electric system properly. *No.*

He raced into the kitchen and closed the hatch to the water system and shut the pantry door.

It's two hundred years. Don't waste time. None of it will be usable by then, no matter what I do.

"Jerry!" Lil shrieked.

He raced back. She had a bundle of clothes in her arms and from the light spilling out of the copper room, there were signs of animals rattling the front door of the house.

"Get inside!" She needed no extra encouragement.

The last thing he saw before he closed the copper door was a window breaking and dozens of brown and white mottled rats spilling into the house.

He shut the air-tight door and pulled the locking lever.

Scratches started on the door.

"Can they get through?"

"Probably not the door, but given enough time, they could claw their way through the walls or ceiling. We won't give them that time."

She nodded agreement.

He turned the dial back to the mark he'd left after their first big time shift.

"Twenty seconds gave us a hundred and fifty years or so. Thirty seconds?"

She nodded, and started a stopwatch application on her cell phone. "Anything to stop that scratching."

He flipped the switch and she tapped her phone.

The scratching was silenced, replaced by that same high-pitched, ragged tone.

"What is that sound?" she asked.

Before he could make a guess, the raggedness got worse, much worse, with the sound almost dropping out for a couple of seconds. Then it came back, stronger.

Lil held up her phone. "Twenty-five seconds. Twenty-eight, Twenty-nine, thirty."

He flipped the switch. The silence was deafening.

Year 394

They stood in silence, not really wanting to check outside, to see what they had just done. From the equipment rack, there was a click and a hiss, as the automatic air system made a small adjustment.

"I guess..."

She nodded. "Go ahead."

He unsealed the door and opened it a crack. It was bright daylight outside. Strong sunlight. The roof of the house and most of the walls were gone. He opened it wider. The copper room was the only structure standing in the ruins of a house long burned to the ground.

A red sheep poked its nose around a crumbling half wall. It bleated in surprise, and ducked back out of sight.

. . .

"Did you see that?" she asked.

"A red sheep. I've seen goats with red hair, but never a sheep with red wool. Do you think someone dyed it."

She pushed past him and walked across the rubble that had been the floor of the house. It was now uneven dirt, with weeds poking their way up through the stones.

The house, or the ruins of the house, was the centerpiece of the walled corral. Their fellow inhabitants were nine red sheep. The iron gate was down, rusting a few yards away, but a log fence had been constructed to keep the sheep in their pen. There was a leather-lined water trough against the wall and a pile of hay that seemed just slightly more interesting to the sheep than the strange humans that had come to join them.

"Eww. Jerry, watch where you step."

He was poking under the copper room with a stick.

"What are you doing?" she asked.

"I built this room, with my uncle. We stripped it down to the foundation and wall studs and rebuilt it. I think that during the time we were frozen, the whole room must have settled a couple of inches as the wooden parts of the foundation burned or rotted away. I didn't feel it happen, did you?"

She grabbed his arm. "My stomach was so fluttery the whole time we could have fallen off a cliff and I wouldn't have noticed it.

She pulled him up. "Come on back inside. We're awake, so this is morning, and I need breakfast."

One of the sheep tried to follow them, but he firmly shut the door in its face.

"Sit down." He did, while she prepared a flat, but sweet pastry from the Park Regat's food bag.

"So, we're two hundred years farther into the future."

He nodded, chewing. "About that, or maybe a little more. I've got an idea."

His laptop had a music program. He opened it up and started tapping the piano keys. "Stop me when you hear the same tone that we heard while time traveling." He worked his way up the scale.

"Stop. Go back one." She was listening with her eyes closed.

He tapped the selected note several times. "Yes, I'm not terribly musical, but I think that's close," he agreed.

He dug into the menus and said, "That's a 'F' in the seventh octave, or about 2800 cycles per second." He looked at her to get her reaction as he talked it out.

"I'm thinking that the copper room isn't perfectly impervious. Some things can get through, especially if they take their time. As the day goes from a hot day to a cold night, maybe the room itself expands and contracts just a little. If we were traveling 2800 days per second, then we might hear a tone like that."

"And when it fluttered..."

"Then those were the days and weeks when it was overcast and the temperature was relatively constant."

"Um, Jerry. This last time, there was a second or two when the sound stopped."

"And it was louder just after that. So probably that was when the house burned down, and we got more direct sunlight."

He had a theory about the silence, but he didn't want to voice it yet.

"We have people living here."

"Shepherds, "he nodded. "Which brings up another question?"

"What's that?"

"When we meet our neighbors, are you my wife, my lover, or my sister?"

"What?"

He was solemn. "It has to be one of those. In the vast majority of the cultures of history, the girl was some kind of property. If we're in one of those, then "just friends" isn't going to cut it. If this is a matriarchy, then we can swap roles in a flash, but the same relationships would hold. We just need to keep our story straight."

She frowned at first. "Abraham and Sarah." She nodded. "He passed Sarah off as his sister at first, when he met this king, to avoid getting killed. It was a bad idea and they had to fess up when the king noticed he was being cursed by God."

She took his hand. "I'm willing to pretend we're married, if you are."

"No problem."

"But pretend in public only."

He agreed. It meant more difficult nights ahead, but this is what he signed up for.

"Do we wait for the shepherd to show up, or do we go searching for a village?"

          ...

Keeping the copper room a secret seemed the safest idea. The weather was warm, but they might be out over night, so he wore his jacket and she dressed in her long dress and they packed limited food and brought only their charged cell phones. As a phone, they were useless, but they could be flashlights and cameras. The clocks were no longer corrected by a radio network, but they still ticked away sixty seconds to the minute, so they were useful time pieces.

They had nothing like weapons, not even a pocket knife. He brought the knife, fork, and spoon from his picnic supplies. He might have some use for them, here in the year 2400. Thus far, the technology level, other than the red sheep, looked no different from that in 2400 BC.

The copper room door had no outside lock, but it did have a handle. He shut down the electricity to conserve the battery and then closed the door and wedged a stick through the handle to keep it reasonably airtight. Surely the shepherds and many others over the centuries had tried that handle and confirmed that it wouldn't budge. If they didn't see anything different, they weren't likely to try again, and discover the secrets within.

He piled a fallen tree branch against the door to obscure his make-do latch. It would have to be enough.

"Are you ready?"

"How far are we going?" Lil looked at the door and he could tell that she was having second thoughts.

He looked at the sun. "It's noonish, and we're really not prepared for camping. Let's head towards downtown for a while. If nothing shows up, we'll come back here and try again, with an early morning start and a better idea of the landscape outside. Okay?"

"Okay." They eased through the gate, making sure that the red sheep stayed put.

For the first time since they left their home time behind, they were outside the stone wall. The landscape was different from the forest of two centuries ago. There were maples and oak and many birch trees. Those were spread out enough so their branches had a wide reach, with ancient blackened stumps telling of a time when their ancestors had shaded the ground. From time to time as they walked down the path they remembered as Montecello street, a weathered pile of bricks and stones poked knee high above the grass. The street followed a rise towards downtown. Off in the distance, a flock of sheep, mostly white with an occasional black one, were grazing. Their shepherd was sitting quietly under a tree. He paid them no mind. Jerry made a mental note of his clothes, dirty-white shirt and pants, with a leather belt and a bag on the ground beside him. It was nothing like his jeans and jacket, but there was nothing he could do about it.

"I'd hate to try to farm this land." Jerry kicked at a curbstone that had survived centuries longer than the street crews who cast it could have imagined. "A plow would always be overturning the remnants of city structures."

"How far have we gone?" she asked. "I thought it was just the house that burned down, but it must have been a forest fire."

"Or worse."

"Worse?"

"I'm just guessing, but you remember that gap of silence, a few decades after we left the Mutagenic Park?"

"Yes. What happened? Did the sun stop shining?"

He nodded. "That's what makes sense."

She shivered. "What could possibly make the sun stop for ..." she did some multiplication in her head, "... for a dozen years?"

"I've read theories. Back in the days when everyone thought Russia and the US were going to nuke each other and kill off billions of people, there was a theory called Nuclear Winter. The idea was that the nukes would throw so much dust into the air that it would blot out the sun for years, and freeze the planet."

She shivered. He picked up a pebble and looked at it—a fragment of an old red brick, weathered smooth. He sent it skipping across the dirt ahead of them.

"Well, other scientists took the same idea, only looking at the effects of other disasters, like asteroid impacts or massive lava flows like the ones in India millions of years ago. This forest fire we see may have been just a part of something that covered the continent or maybe the whole world, filling the sky with clouds that blocked out the sun for a decade.

"Or at least enough so that we couldn't hear the flicker of the sunlight."

"At least the trees came back. And the grass," she said.

"And people. Don't forget the people. People survived. But I don't know about the technology, or the culture. All we've seen is evidence of sheep herding."

She walked a little closer to him. "So don't expect the Park Regat to drive up and give us a ride."

"Probably not."

The path had dropped into a gully, and the trees were thicker, but as they reached the flat meadows, the Mississippi River came into view. There were buildings visible. But none were the ones they remembered. This was barely a village. There were tilled fields, but that was hardly different from their own time. Only now, the residential streets and businesses of downtown Canton were no longer visible.

Jerry pointed uphill, "The only stone building in sight. I bet this place floods."

"Canton was always in danger of flooding. Remember the levees?" She pointed. "They've moved. A different position from my time, but they're still here."

Lil pulled him on, "And that looks like a marketplace." They walked on another half mile.

Suddenly, she stopped still. She looked upstream, and then towards the closest point to the river, and then to the right and the left. She was almost spinning in place.

"Lil?" He put out his hand and stopped her. "What's up?"

"I...I know where I am." She pointed. "That's where the school was. And that's where our church was. And that's where Casey's was where I bought donuts." Her eyes were shiny. It was hitting, all at once. He put his arm around her.

A woman came out of a nearby hut. Her home, he guessed. She came close.

"Zi Dam feel'n ill?"

He shook his head. "She'll be okay."

His words caught her attention, perhaps his accent. "Lake-ins?"

Lil tried to put a smile on her face. She tidied up the moisture around her eyes. Her voice started weak, then cleared. "Thank you. But I'm fine."

The lady said something rapidly. Jerry was sure it was English, a version of it, but he couldn't follow it when she spoke fast. All he could do was smile and nod.

Lil gripped his arm. "Did you say church?"

The lady nodded and mumbled some more words and pointed to the stone building on the hill.

Lil turned to him and whispered. "That's the local church. She says we can get help there."

"Do you want to risk it? No telling what religion is dominant here."

She looked at him with limited patience. "You want to know what people are like? Check out the churches."

He nodded. He didn't have as much confidence in the church as she did, but she wasn't wrong.

They climbed the hill and he got a good look at the building. It was hardly the white steeples of his age, but it was still the largest structure around. Maybe eighty feet on the long side, with two small windows visible. The door was wood. The roof was peaked, built of trimmed logs and capped with peat. The stones from which it was built had been scavenged from all around. He could see old brick, limestone, and granite boulders and even chunks of concrete.

There was a thin curl of smoke from a small chimney in the rear. Although his instincts demanded caution, he knocked on the door. They waited, nervously looking around.

The door opened and an old man in a white shirt and dark trousers and a black cloth wrapped around his neck greeted them. The words were quick and again, Lil caught them better than he could. "We're travelers," she said.

The cleric frowned. "Zi Lake-ins?"

Jerry shook his head. These people didn't like Lake-ins. He understood that much. He spoke very slowly.

"We are very far from home. I don't know who Lake-ins are."

The man peered far upriver, and then nodded and smiled. "Please come in."

He lit an oil lantern and seated them on a straight wooden bench at a table where they could talk. The inside of the church building had pews of the same wooden benches, with seating for a hundred or so, depending on how cozy everyone was.

"I am Speaker Joseph." He spoke slowly, as if trying to match how his visitors had spoken. Jerry relaxed a bit. "Where are you from?"

Jerry had been giving his story some thought.

"We are traveling, exiled from our home. We are so lost I can't even point in the direction we are from. We just recently came from the west. This is the first we've seen of the river."

"From your words, you sound almost like those from far upriver, the Lake-ins, who pass this way in ships. They raid our town. I apologize if your welcome has been tainted by our suspicions."

"No one has treated us badly, and we certainly have no claim on you."

Lil had been staying reasonably silent, trying to get a feel for a woman's place. Timidly, she asked, "We were wondering which God you worshiped."

The Speaker smiled. "We bow before the one God and Jesu his son who is risen."

She revealed a small pocket Bible she had been keeping out of sight. "This is mine."

He looked at it and beamed as he saw the cross on its cover. "Our people welcome you as sister and brother."

Timidly, he asked, "May I hold it?"

She presented it to him.

He was impressed by the embossed leather cover, but when he opened it up and saw the thin pages and tiny print, he paused and rubbed his finger tips on his shirt to clean them.

After a careful sampling of the pages, he asked, "Is this...the whole Bible?"

She nodded, "Sixth-six books."

He was overwhelmed. "I had thought it was just a totem. A cross to hold. But when I opened it up..." He held a page up to the weak light. "My old eyes would need sunlight to read this, but it's a marvel. Where did you get this?"

Lil glanced at Jerry. She didn't know how much to reveal. He gestured toward the book.

"I purchased one just like that in a town called La Grange just last year. But that was before our exile. I wouldn't have any idea who would be able to produce this type of book now."

Speaker Joseph chuckled, "There's a La Grange just down river from us. I wish I could buy a Bible. The pages I inherited from my predecessor are just holding together."

Reluctantly, he handed the pocket Bible back to Lil.

"Where are you traveling to?"

Lil looked at him again. Jerry shrugged. "It's a difficult question."

She looked down at her hands. "If we could find a way back from exile...I would go home in an instant, even with all the difficulties I'd face. But that may not be possible..."

Jerry sighed. "From all I know, our exile is permanent. If I could find a way to make it happen..."

Speaker Joseph shook his head. "When a soldier is exiled from his homeland, and returns, he's generally considered an enemy."

"You're probably right." He took Lil's hand. "So my goal right now is to find a place where Lil can live a safe, happy life. I'm her protector, and that's my number one purpose in life."

She smiled back, but through the sadness of their exile.

"So, you haven't chosen a destination?"

"No. What places do you know about?"

The old preacher leaned back and thought a moment.

"You could always find a piece of land and make it your own. You wouldn't have to walk more than an hour from here to find good soil free for the taking."

Jerry's face showed a twisted smile. "I've no experience farming. We'd probably starve before I could learn how."

Joseph waved his hand, "Oh, I understand. Someone with your skills, education and training can seek much higher. I'm just pointing out that a quiet life is possible."

Lil said, "We may choose that, but there are options we have to search out first."

"I understand. Now...how familiar are you with the Kingdoms of the River?"

...

Before too long they had a mini tutorial on the geopolitics of mid-North America. Speaker Joseph was also the local school teacher, and three of the Canton area families had put their elder children in his care, to learn to read and write, and to learn the basics of the world. Jerry and Lil were just two more students to a well-worn lecture.

The local superpower was the Lake People, Lake-ins, who lived on the shore of Lake Michigan, roughly where Chicago was. In addition to lake commerce, they controlled the Illinois River to Sloo, which Jerry took to be St. Louis, and the Mississippi river from Sloo to Rock Island. The kings of Northern Illinois owed fealty to the King of the Lake People, but the three kings on the western side of the river didn't—which made Canton fair game to the traders who plied the circle trade controlled by the Lake-ins.

From Rock Island, loggers and trappers made log barges to carry furs and grain south to Sloo. Along the way, they would raid the western shore to pick up slaves. At Sloo, they would trade slaves and cargo with merchants that controlled the lower Mississippi. The log barges would also be sold off and the Lake-ins traders would return to their home on the lake with south-land supplies using their three prized steam ships that never left the protected waters of the Illinois River.

Speaker Joseph knew little about the Ohio River lands, other than the rumors that the Lake-ins bought the steam ships from people in the East. He was aware of the mountains to the west, but there was little trade in that direction.

"And I know nothing of the down river kingdoms. No one I know has ever returned when taken to slavery that direction."

"Has anyone returned?"

"Oh, yes. Speak to Three-fingered James. He was gone to slavery for five years. He was taken to the Lake and took the cross land journey to Rock Island and came back on a raft. He jumped free when he reached us and is fearful for his life if they ever catch him again. But he has many fine tales to tell of the Lake People."

He pointed to Jerry, "You might actually find fortune in the Lake lands, with your skills. But you," he pointed to Lil, "must make every effort to stay out of sight if a Lake-ins barge is sighted. Women taken to slavery are not treated lightly. If the call is sounded, get up here, inside these stone walls with the other women and the children and we can barricade the doors. Perhaps they could breach them, but they don't usually spend the time. They snatch the unwary and are off down river before we can chase them."

She shivered. "I don't think I would like that."

Jerry nodded, "I don't think I could let that happen. Besides, we are just grateful for the learning you have shared. Perhaps we should be heading back to the last place we camped, far from the river."

Joseph rose, "Oh, please stay! There is a corner over there with straw and a blanket where you could spend the night. Tomorrow at the second hour is our Sunday worship and many would love to meet you."

Lil looked at him and nodded slightly. He sighed, "Okay, but we must move on soon."

"Wonderful! I will arrange for your supper. Besides, you young people probably need some fresh air. These lamps are a comfort to me, but the air gets stuffy."

Speaker Joseph hurried down hill, anxious to share the news. Lil and Jerry sat on a stone perch overlooking the town.

Lil whispered, "Sorry I turned down the chance to learn farming."

"I would have done so if you hadn't. This looks like a nice place, but even before I knew about the slave raids, I had a feeling living here would lead to a short lifespan. If not for us, then for our kids. Poor diet and limited medicine is a given in conditions like this. We had to come and check out the culture, but I'd vote in an instant to move forward in time, and find a more technologically advanced era, where you would have a chance to survive childbirth."

"You're worried about my kids aren't you?"

He grumbled, "Kids come from sex, and I'm not getting any until your safety is covered."

She looked stunned for an instant, then covered it by pointing down hill. "Looks like the word is out. Visitors are coming."

. . .

The feast was spontaneous. Food began arriving, as well as a constant stream of villagers. Lil was swept away instantly to talk with the women. The men had other concerns.

"Zi fought raiders before?" asked one of the men milling around at the viewpoint. A few other eyes turned from peering upriver to see what he had to say.

Why ask me? he thought, until he suddenly had a feeling that his letterman jacket had a distinct military look in their eyes. Obviously they'd never seen anything like it before. Maybe they thought he was a soldier.

"Ah, tell me how these raiders fight."

Someone called for James, and a slight man who kept his left hand tucked into his waistband, came forward. He was their expert.

"The river don't stop. Raiders know they got a short time to get ashore, grab someone and get back. You can catch up at a run, but a struggling man or a copse of trees in the wrong place could leave them stranded. That's why they risk lashing the barge to a dock, even though they know it's dangerous.

"A double handful. That's all there were on the barge that caught me, and more men that are here tonight to stop 'em. But they had me by both arms, threw me on the barge and were off, in hardly the time it takes to tell it."

Once they were in motion, there was nothing the townspeople could do to rescue him. James was just one of a half-dozen slaves that were picked up on the journey south. One or two captives per try was considered excellent work. Towns with good warning systems appeared deserted and not worth the effort, although the raiders would occasionally torch a few houses just to vent their frustration if a village was regularly vacant.

Barge operators talked to each other, and sometimes two or three crews would dock together and make an example of an obstinate town. If the whole town was being burned, hidden farmers would appear to fight, and the chances of a rich capture was high.

Jerry asked, "Why do you even have a dock? It makes it easier for the raiders."

They had to sell their crops. At the right season, they would fly a white flag, and a barge operator who had capacity and trade goods available would dock and they would negotiate. Sometimes a barge who had taken slaves just the year before made a good trading partner if the market was right. Plus, the village was prepared at that time, with a crew of men to load the cargo, and to fight if necessary to keep everything honest.

Jerry tried to hold off talking about his own military experience, which was non-existent outside of books. They wondered at his reluctance, but his education had given him some ideas. He just needed more time to think about it.

The feast didn't last long after sunset. No one wanted to be out and visible when raiders could sneak up in the dark. It was the season and they'd survived two raids thus far and everyone felt that their luck couldn't hold.

Speaker Joseph showed them to their corner and gave them a red wool blanket.

As the last light winked out and their host retired to his quarters at the other end of the building, Lil and Jerry struggled with making the best of their bedding.

He put his arms around her. "How did your day go?" he whispered.

She wiggled a little closer and he had to brush her hair out of his eyes.

"You know I've always been small, well, it's different here. Did you notice that they think you're a giant?"

"A giant?" He had noticed that everyone was smallish, and come to think of it, he was larger than them all, but it hadn't occurred to him that he was unusual. On the basketball team, his six foot two was on the small side. "It's probably the diet. I've read that modern Americans have increasingly gotten larger than their ancestors because we had the best food supply, not because of our genetics."

"Jerry, I kinda think 'Modern American' might not mean much any more. Not for us."

"Right."

"Anyway, I want to report that romance hasn't gone out of the imaginations of girls in four hundred years. You should have heard the speculation! One of the girls my age, married with two kids by the way, thinks I'm a princess and you're a palace guard who stole me away, and we're on the run from my father's soldiers. I have to be a princess because of my fancy clothes.

"Of course, I'm not on everyone's friend list. My skirt is way too short, according to an aunt of hers. It shows skin. If I stayed here, I'd have to get a new outfit that skims the dirt, or good men would start having evil thoughts. I can't imagine what they'd think of my cheerleader outfit." She chuckled. "Of course, I'm not the only disruptive influence around here."

"Oh?"

"Yes, I got asked about you. Since you're a giant and all. Is everything large? Is your...?"

"Hey! None of that. Not here. Not now."

"I'm just saying. You've caught a few eyes. Of course, I had to confess that I really had no standard for comparison."

"Cut that out." He wasn't kidding. The role they were playing made it hard enough.

"So," he asked. "What do you think of this version of Canton?"

She was quiet for a moment. "I can't help but imagine that these are my relatives. I know—four hundred years is a long time. But I keep thinking—maybe those eyes are the same as Meg's. Maybe her hair is the same shade as my mother's. You know?"

"Not really. I was noticing all the differences. We have the whitest skin around. The good old American melting pot has stirred the mix for a while. And there are some real differences too."

"I know! Did you see the family with all the hair? I mean it's attractive and all, but if that blonde girl was back in our time, she'd be called a werewolf."

"That's what they say here, too. It's the Peters family. I was talking with one of the guys about the raiders and the people they grabbed as slaves, and Caleb said his grandfather, John Peters, was a werewolf and he felt slavers would seek out him and his family because they could charge more for them."

"Seriously?"

"Seriously. The guys mentioned my white skin too, and we were talking about differences. People with fur are rare, but not supernatural or anything. It has to be a result of that mutagenic stuff."

"I think that's over with. I was talking with a girl who had her kids with her and she warned them to be good, or the shape-changers would come after them. When I asked her about it later, she said it was just one of those old fairytales, and wasn't real."

"Maybe no new changes, but there are definitely some new variations in the gene pool—werewolves and red sheep and giant turtles."

"I didn't hear about those."

"Yep. I was warned to keep my distance from the river unless I could swim really fast. Supposedly there are some snappers that can take your leg off. Dangerous, but excellent eating."

"Jerry. What do you think about this place?"

"I don't know. This slavery business is upsetting. They live in fear because of it. They can't really get any help from their king, because it's such a random thing. The king can't station guards all along the river. He'd be spread too thin. And the villagers can't afford to take time out of the day-to-day grind to develop their own military. It's a no win situation. They depend on the very people who prey on them."

"It sounds like you've been thinking about this."

"They think I'm some kind of soldier. My letter jacket is a uniform. They're asking my help. They want me to suggest some new foreign tactics they can use."

"Can you tell them you're not a soldier?"

"I don't think they'd listen to me. They *believe* I'm the soldier come to rescue them. You can hear it in the way they talk. They need to believe it."

She tugged his arms a little tighter around her. "I believe it. You're big and strong and smart. Of course you're a soldier. You're a prince in exile."

He heard the tiredness in her voice. He held her gently. She'd be asleep soon, but his brain was churning over all those books he'd read. Surely there was something he could remember that could help this little powerless group of farmers to keep the raiders at bay.

...

Lil woke as the dawn pink began leaking in through the little windows. She felt for the warmth of Jerry's arms but there was nothing but hay. Like the still mirror of a silent lake is churned by the first breeze, her dreams fragmented beyond recall.

She whispered his name. Nothing. She found her feet and draped the red blanket around her shoulders and began her search.

Jerry looked up as she found him on the lookout stone, staring off at the river, murky with the morning fog.

"Hi."

"Morning. I'm glad you're here. This is your town. Do you remember much about the lock and dam?"

He was all business. She wondered if he'd slept much.

She looked off at the line stretched across the water. "I remember the ones in my time. It was Lock and Dam Number twenty, of about thirty. But this one is different design. I guess things have changed over the centuries. And this version looks worse for wear."

There were two obvious gaps in the ancient structure; a big span near the middle of the river, and a smaller one a bit closer. With the remnants of the old locks right next to town, with the gates long gone, that made three places large enough for a log barge to pass.

He stood up and faced her, adjusting the drape of the blanket around her shoulders. "I'm going to walk down to the dam and take a look at their dock. Will you be okay here by yourself?"

She reached out with one hand and set her palm on the letter of his jacket. "You be careful. You'd make a prime slave yourself. And remember, church service is this morning."

"I'll remember." He smiled and kissed her forehead. "Don't worry. Remember what this is for." He fingered the little running figure on his jacket next to the basketball and the baseball. "800 meter district champion. I can outrun any river pirate."

...

The river was running a little faster than he remembered, probably because it was forced through the gaps in the dam. Long before he was born, a whole chain of low dams were built across the Mississippi with locks for the barge traffic. It kept the river navigable from Minnesota to the Gulf of Mexico year around, except for the most severe dry spells.

What he could see of the dam showed concrete with places where bones of rebar iron poked through. How many years had passed since this version of the dam had last seen any service? Surely there were yearly floods that topped the whole span. In a way Jerry was surprised that any of it was left. Maybe materials engineering had advanced beyond his day.

At the lock, he could see massive hinges that had been bent and nearly pulled free. The heavy gates, that had held back the current while barges moved through, were long gone. They were probably miles downstream, buried under the mud.

He'd lived on the Mississippi and knew the dredges that had kept the official channel nine feet deep for barge traffic. He suspected that any clear channel was long gone, silted in. These pirate barges had to stay shallow draft and keep a crew working to pole clear of sand bars. Three-fingered James had mentioned long days of being roped to the side of his captor's barge, pole in hand, working to keep it moving in the current. In difficult stretches, the barge would be roped off to a tree on the shore overnight so that sharp eyes could direct its course during the daylight.

Canton's dock was just a little walk downstream from the old locks, in this time built right on the levee. The little park he remembered was long gone, and there used to be a small side-channel that was missing. But that wasn't surprising. The riverbed shifted. It always had. It did seem that the river was higher on the levee than he'd seen it before in his home time. Was this normal, or just the rainy season?

He looked at the dock's position, relative to the dam. Any barge coming to raid or trade would have to come through the locks. It would be difficult or impossible for the raft to shoot through the gaps in the center of the river and make it back to shore before the current would have swept them long past the dock.

If this weren't an agricultural community that depended on trade, filling in the old locks and demolishing the dock would make them relatively secure from raids. But this wasn't an era where they could load their cargo on wagons and truck it to another port town.

Echoing across the town came a haunting call. He looked around. Up on the observation rock by the church, a young man was repeating a slow chant. *Da. Da. Dama. Da.* It repeated several times. It was probably words, but he couldn't make them out. People were leisurely coming out of their houses and making their way up the hill.

Oh good. It was the call to worship, not a raider alert. In other times and places, it would have been a church bell. Well, he promised Lil he'd be there on time, so he brushed the old rust off his hands he'd accumulated when he looked at the locks and started back to the hill at a brisk pace.

...

The women sat on the right side of the pews and the men on the left. Speaker Joseph sat on the front bench and Lil was already seated with a group of women mostly her age, with little ones in their laps. Jerry caught sight of some of the men he'd talked with at the feast and they made room for him.

Before anyone stood up to direct the service, a song began.

"Take time to be holy. Speak up with zi Lord."

Jerry felt a shiver. He'd intended to sit quietly, just to listen and show his solidarity with these people. He hadn't intended to hear a song he'd last sung himself just a few days earlier.

On the other side of the room, in a clear trained voice, he heard Lil join in.

"Abide in Him always, and feed on his Word."

He couldn't help himself. He wasn't a singer, not trained, not in any choir of any type, but his mouth opened and he sang.

"Make friends of God's children. Help those who are weak."

Yes, Lil and he sang slightly different words, but the eyes that turned their way showed a recognition that yes, they were all the same, God's children.

. . .

There were prayers. What looked to be Speaker Joseph's apprentice read scriptures from single sheets of paper carefully held as if they were on the verge of crumbling to dust. The Speaker told the story of the angel that visited Abraham to tell him that old Sarah his wife would have a child. When he mentioned the part where Sarah, overhearing the visitor laughed, Jerry had the feeling that maybe the subtext was that the villagers shouldn't make fun of the strangers in their midst.

There was more singing, lots more singing. Singing just for the fun of it. Since most of the songs seemed to start spontaneously, Lil was tempted to start one of her own. It was one of those great solo pieces that Jerry didn't even know the words to, and none of the others did either. Even so, there were a few voices joining in as they started to recognized the chorus. Lil had a great voice and soon some of the others were showing their stuff as well.

By the time the service ended, everyone felt like life-long friends. Jerry sensed it too. Why would he be so surprised to find such a familiar group? It was only four hundred years, and groups like this had been singing together for thousands of years before his time.

. . .

Most of the same group he'd talked to the night before gathered by the observation stone after people began departing down the hill.

"So, Lord Jereomy, zi have thoughts about fighting raiders?" James asked. It wasn't a casual question anymore.

He walked to the edge and pointing down, asked, "How many times does the levee flood?"

They conferred. "It happens."

Wilson, a bald-headed man with a sour face said, "That's my pasture right next to the levee. Flooded six times since I last rebuilt the house."

Jerry directed the next question to him. "I have to ask. Which is a worse disaster, to have the levee flood, or to have the slavers take someone away?"

He shook his head and brushed his scalp as if he had hair. He looked at the ground. "I hate the muck, but both my boys are gone to slavers. When James here made it back, I had hope for a year or so, but now I don't think I'll ever see them again."

He looked Jerry in the eye, anger in his voice. "I'd flood to the forests to keep the Lake-ins from taking anyone else!"

Jerry nodded. To the group he said, "There might be a way. You see, the raiders are just passing through, catching a ride on the current. But you people, this town, you *own* this part of the river. You just have to prove it to them."

...

Lil brought her man his lunch. "Jerry, get over here, and put your shirt back on. You're turning red."

He set down the woven bucket full of dirt and rocks and looked up at her. "Stand back, I'll get mud on your new dress."

She watched her bare-chested giant climb up the rise next to the old locks and wished she dared let him get close. He was covered in sweat. Instead she held out her new white skirt and twirled. "Isn't it lovely! Sheila's aunt, I mentioned her, said I needed a proper dress and so she gave me one."

Holding out his shirt at full arm's length, she waited until he put it back on and asked him, "What are you doing here?" There were six of them, digging away at a section of the levee. There were a pile of logs that she'd seen another crew haul across from the tree line. None of the women she was chatting with knew what was going on. When Sheila offered to supply her with Jerry's lunch, she grabbed at the chance to come down to the work site. Other women were arriving as well and the excavation was grinding to a temporary halt.

Jerry mumbled, "Helping those who are weak."

"What?"

"Just a song stuck in my head. What did you bring me?" He reached into the basket.

She slapped his hand. "You can spare a splash of water to get the mud off you fingers, or you'll be eating it." She poured and he scrubbed his hands together.

"Now you can eat." It was corn dumplings, with a hint of mutton broth. Jerry found it surprisingly good.

Lil munched on one daintily, "Now, what are you doing? It's a big mystery up on the hill."

He grinned. "Military secret. Or hair-brained scheme. One or the other. Only don't tell them the last part."

"Well, don't flood the town by accident. We're living on good will as it is."

"Lil, I need you to do something for us."

"Oh?"

"See this flagpole." She looked suspiciously at the rough, twenty-foot tall tree trunk, just trimmed of branches, standing there on the levee. She nodded.

"Terry's middle boy climbs to the top of that every season when the town has goods to trade and hangs a white flag. It's the sign to the barge operators that the town wants to do business. I want a different flag flying here to warn them to steer clear. Some other color that they'll see."

She looked at the other people. "I don't know if you've noticed, but they're weak on colors here. White wool and cotton, and they're good making some black dye out of sumac leaves, I think, but not much else. Oh! What about that red blanket? They've got natural red wool."

He nodded. "Blood red wool. Yes, that might be the perfect thing. Can you make it happen? I really need that flag flying as soon as possible."

. . .

James set the basket of swords down with a clatter.

"Let's see what you've got." Jerry picked through the collection quickly. Five machete-like blades made of copper or bronze. He flexed one just enough to tell how strong it was. It wasn't. The edges were nicked and gouged. The sixth, the jewel of the lot, was plain ugly.

Someone long past had found a piece of rebar steel and had beaten it flat. It had an edge, but it was hardly sharp. Handles on them all were just wrapped leather. There were no guards.

James explained. "Most of these were lost by raiders over time. They don't get much use. The raiders come, and we run and hide. I didn't run fast enough." He idly rubbed at the stumps of the two missing fingers on his left hand. His masters had taken the smaller fingers so he could still do a good days work with a solid grip.

"I think you're right, James. The axes are in much better shape."

"Paid a good price for them too. Nearly a season's worth of red wool. And copper, not iron. They don't sell iron on this side of the river."

Terry grumbled. "I found that long one, but the woman wouldn't let me keep it. Fighting's for the devils, she says. No offense." He apologized.

"None taken." Jerry nodded, "The best fighting is far away, where your wife and kids don't even know it's happening. Live your life growing things, making things with your hands, and helping your neighbors."

There was a murmur of approval. They all wished for that. It didn't stop them from looking upriver from time to time. It was an ingrained habit. A survival skill.

"I want to be clear. I'm not staying here." There were nods. These eight men were the real government of the place. Speaker Joseph steered their souls and King Ben of Macon claimed the lands, but these men who had asked for his help and listened to his plan and spent the day digging with him, they spoke and people did as they were told.

"My woman and I have to move on soon, maybe in a day or so. But I'll spend every waking breath trying to help. I know a lot about metalwork, and I can give some instruction, if there's someone who is willing to listen. If I had a month and willing hands I could make swords better than any of these. And more than swords. Iron axes. Shields that could turn aside a raider's sword. Iron plows. Iron nails. Saws and tools to craft your wood into hundreds of shapes.

"But it will take a man with strong muscles who can dedicate a whole lifetime to the craft."

He pointed across the river. "Over there, blacksmiths build these things and give their farmers more power over the soil and their carpenters and weavers the ability to make finer things for their wives.

"And the Lake-ins don't want you to know these things. They want you to live your life just like yesterday and the day before, so that they can take your crops and your wool and your children for themselves and hear no objection from you when they come calling.

"Speaker Joseph has been teaching you Bible all your lives." There were nods and a chuckle.

"Well, let me tell you a secret that my Speaker told me. The Canaanites had chariots of iron and the giant Goliath had a spear tipped with iron. The Israelites had only copper and a few iron tools that they had captured from others." He plucked the iron sword out of the basket. "Until David. With his reign, the Israelites could make iron tools and iron weapons of their own. And then, David's nation became great. Whether God chose David to bring iron to his people or not is beyond my wisdom, but if you have a young man who is quick to learn and has the strength to hold a hammer, I need to talk to him."

...

Jerry nearly dozed off when the sun went down. Lil sat down beside him by the fire. Most of the men had let him rest, and she was reluctant to wake him, but she didn't want him to catch a chill.

He stirred. "Hi."

"Are you okay?"

He smiled. "Yeah, fine. It's just been a very long day."

"I saw you lecturing. I didn't know you were a teacher. What did you tell them? History?"

"Very little of that. I wouldn't know what to say. I missed out on most of theirs. No, I was teaching blacksmithing, verbally, which is a joke."

"Oh?"

"Sure. That's the kind of thing you need hands on experience, and they don't have any of the tools. No forge and bellows. No coal. No iron. It was all theoretical. I talked a good game, but they may not ever make anything of it."

He rubbed his forehead, and she moved around to massage his shoulders. She asked, "Is it important?"

"Oh yes! This trick with the levee and the barges may...*may* give them some relief from the raiders, but until they make the jump from tools they buy from the Lake-ins, to tools they make for themselves, they will continue to be just prey.

"They have one fact on their side. There is iron littered all over the place. Every place where there used to be concrete, there's rebar iron for the taking. Old house foundations, sidewalks, parking lots. Places like that. They've been collecting 'hard roots' and tossing them into the river as they worked their fields. They won't have to learn how to smelt iron from ore for a long time to come—which is lucky, because I'm not sure I know enough of the details to teach them."

"Are you done for the night?"

He sighed, "I guess so. Speaker Joseph's apprentice Samuel? He was in the classes taking notes. I want to have some time with him to make sure he got the facts straight. When we're gone, their memories and his notes will be all that they have. For sure, the Lake-ins won't share."

"Then I think you should come on to bed. Get some sleep."

He nodded and got to his feet.

Lil led the way, holding his hand. "So you think we'll be heading out soon?"

"It's what we agreed on, isn't it?"

"I don't think we did, but you're probably right. You were concerned about my hypothetical kids, and now I am too." She shook her head sadly. "Infant mortality is through the roof here, and mothers dying in childbirth is a common thing. Lots of these kids are being raised by aunts and uncles. As callous as it makes me feel, I think driving down the road a few more decades to where there's decent hospitals would be my choice for a place to settle down."

He shook the hay around to make a softer bed. "Did I imagine it? This blanket is brown, not red."

She turned off the lantern and settled down beside him. "Your red flag, remember?"

But he had already gone to sleep. She shuffled closer, hoping for his arms around her, but he was out, really out. She kissed his cheek and tucked the blanket around them. They hay was itchy. She wanted a real bed. Soon.

...

Dawn came too soon. Jerry woke with his arms around Lil. She was still asleep and he was barely alert. It was the most natural thing in the world to feel her breathing through her dress, and wish he could get more. They were married in this world, weren't they? Almost?

Lil stirred. She blinked her eyes. "Hey."

He thought about a kiss. The thought was all he had time for.

Someone carrying a lantern hurried in. "Wake up. Everyone! Raiders spotted upriver!"

Jerry was up. He grabbed his jacket and was out the door. Samuel was calling to the town. "Raiders! Raiders!" It was a harsher call than before.

Three-fingered James was on the observation rock, peering out at the mist covered waters. "Two."

Jerry blinked the rest of the sleep from his eyes. Yes, there were two ripples in the mist. The closest was veering towards them, aiming for the lock. It made sense. They were hunting for stragglers with a time limit. A second barge wouldn't likely catch anyone.

The first barge was only three or four minutes away.

Jerry turned and almost knocked Lil down. "Get back inside, and stay there!"

"What are you...?"

"GO!" He started running, down the slope.

James called after him. "I'll make sure she does!"

With a downhill run, his strides were so long he was at the verge of losing his balance, especially on the irregular ground. To his left, families still in nightgowns were struggling uphill to the safety of the church building. A few figures were converging on the lock with him.

Terry got there first and grabbed up the first sword out of the basket hidden behind a bush. Jerry grabbed for the iron sword. Wilson was wheezing, out of breath, but he was the third man in place. He grabbed an axe.

Others were coming, but Jerry had eyes only on the barge. The barge's pilot was calling out orders. Half the men were manning the poles, pushing the barge closer to shore, trying to shoot the gap in the dam without hitting the concrete. Five others were bunched up at the leading edge closest to shore. There were swords among them, and ropes.

James had given him details. The instant they approached the docks, the polers would push the barge up close enough to touch, and binders would loop their lines to the piles of the dock. The binders wouldn't even go ashore, waiting for the signal to loose their lines and shove off with their booty.

"Not this time," he whispered. "Please," he prayed.

The landing party had eyes on them. It was unusual. The farmers usually ran. Some of the attackers were thinking that they might actually have to fight this time.

The leading edge of the barge cleared the lock.

"NOW!" Jerry swung his sword and cut the rope at his feet. Terry and Wilson were doing the same. Terry had to hit twice, but all the lines came free and the trigger log slammed down on the logs they'd wedged into the weakened levee. Like a shovel, the logs lifted the earth and suddenly the water found a new channel, into the farmland sitting a few feet lower than the river's own level. The wash, like a waterfall, pulled the barge. No poling could stop it. The landing party were thrown from their feet and the barge tilted over the gushing water. Some were in the drink.

A wordless battle cry sounded from twenty men behind him. Only a few of the farmers had swords, but there were rakes and poles and tree branches. They all swarmed down onto the raiders, none of which had been able stay upright on their unruly barge as it slammed from side to side in the narrow channel. Quickly, it hit posts, tree stumps, buried in its way. The barge was grounded as the muddy river spilled around it.

The first scream of pain came not from a sword thrust, but from a raider caught under the barge's weight.

Farmers pulled him to the slightly higher ground of Wilson's field, but bound him tight. Those that struggled out of the churning muck, waving their swords, met farmers well able to knock them down time and again, until they lost the will to fight. Before long, most were bound and lying in the dewey green grass, eyeing the rising waters.

Three of the raiders escaped to the levee side, and after a brief exchange, two of them waded into the Mississippi and began swimming toward the other raft nearly a quarter mile away. The other looked fearfully at the water and fearfully at the farmers, and stood his ground.

One man stood defiantly on the remnants of the barge.

Behind them, a rumble caught Jerry's attention. He looked. The second phase had begun as rocks and logs tumbled into the broken gap and experienced men struggled to stop the breach in the levee before it flooded the whole town.

"Soldier!"

Jerry looked back as the last raider charged his way. It occurred to him that the raider's sword looked very nice, well crafted. It was probably very sharp.

The raider glanced at one man after another, growling. Then he caught sight of Jerry's iron sword and his attitude changed. From a charge, he slowed and took a stance, facing the taller man.

This isn't good. Jerry held his sword ready to deflect an attack. He had read books and played video games, but this was entirely different. If this raider was as good as his sword, then Lil might have to find a homeland on her own.

Not my first choice.

The raider ignored everyone else. And the farmers left the swordplay to the soldier/prince-in-exile in their midst. They weren't foolhardy.

'Inside guard', 'outside guard', 'hanging guard'. He'd read those terms, but never quite understood what they meant, and now wasn't the time to regret his ignorance. *Keep from getting hit.* That he understood. He faced the man edge on, to be a smaller target. Holding the sword was the problem. It was heavier than it looked.

The man swung, and Jerry was able to deflect it and return to the guarding position. He took a step back. *Keep some distance, and stay confident.* He was fresh out of bed and a trained athlete, not a man who rode a barge day in and day out.

Clang! Another step back. As he'd hoped, a circle of farmers not dealing with the levee or guarding the bound raiders kept pace with the two of them, giving their attacker limited chance for escape. While he would be happy to see the man head for the hills, he was sure his opponent thought he was fighting for his life.

Jerry shifted his hold on the rebar sword. Somewhere in those books he read, it said not to let your hand cramp. He kept the tip of his sword pointed at the man's right eye. *Clang!* He parried and took

79

a step back. He trusted his companions to warn him if he were about to step on a rock or something. He had to keep his eye forward.

The man lunged, and Jerry's parry was almost not quick enough. There was a second swing that anticipated his move. His leg stung. Had be been nicked? He didn't look down. The man was on attack, and moving closer, getting inside his guard. He stepped back. The raider was ready and lunged again.

Jerry's foot slid off a rock and he was off balance. The fancy blade cut close to his head. Angry, he punched the man's forearm. And the fancy blade went sailing out of the raider's grip.

His fist worked better than the blade so he went with his strength, and clipped the brearded chin with a uppercut, the mass of the sword in hand, giving his punch real impact. The man went down, and Jerry did too, almost kneeling on the man's chest.

Only then did the farmers move in with ropes and bind him.

Jerry used his sword to get back to his feet. Breathing heavily, he realized maybe he wasn't as much a trained athlete as he'd thought. Not when it came to swords. Or maybe it was just reaction from the fight. Nobody had ever tried to kill him before.

When he glanced at the levee, he was amazed to see that the flow was down to a trickle. The wooden lattices they'd piled nearby in preparation must have helped hold the fill in place. He walked back to the barge, now stranded in the mud. The raiders were lined up, looking sullen and fearful.

Two of the men were happy—slaves that had been captured upstream.

"Where are you from?"

"Grayland," said the boy. The older man nodded.

"Can you make it back there?"

They looked at each other. It was plain they didn't know.

Wilson held out his hand, "I'll trade food and a roof for help getting my place back in order. You can leave when you will."

The man nodded and took his hand.

Terry came up and reported. "We'll have the water stopped before noon. What do we do now?"

Jerry had imagined success, but now was the time to see if it played out like he visualized.

"Who is the barge owner?"

Not surprisingly, it was the man he'd fought.

He addressed them all. "Look up at the flag." He pointed at the waving red banner.

"The law of the river has changed! When the red flag is flying, any barge, its cargo, and its crew is forfeit for coming to this town. Take the middle way unless the white trading flag shows. Take a last look at the barge, because it belongs to us now."

There were angry grumbles. One voice asked, "What about us?"

Jerry had a little acting experience and he'd practiced the surprised look he showed.

He rubbed his chin. "Well, the sorry lot of you would make poor slaves. I guess the only other choice is to plant you and grow crops over you...unless. Yes, maybe there's another way.

"You didn't know the law of the river had changed. Probably the other barges don't either. I want you lot," he pointed to a group of five that had been holding poles rather than swords, "unload all the trade goods and stack them there on dry ground. Once that's done, we'll give you enough pieces of this barge to carry the whole smelly lot of you off to Sloo. Be sure to spread the word. This town has no more slaves to give."

He pointed up again. "Red flag, stay away! White flag, come and trade, and we'll trade fairly.

"Now get to work!"

He nodded to Terry. The real boss cut a few ropes and kept the stevedores guarded while they unloaded welcome trade goods.

He whispered to Wilson, "Can you keep an eye on things? I need to go up the hill."

The man gripped his arm. "Thank you. Maybe I'll never see my sons again, but I got a little of my own back, and it felt good."

Jerry waved to the rest of them and trudged his way back up the hill, hiding the pain of his leg. The bleeding wasn't bad, but he had to show no weakness to the raiders. Not after playing the role of the conqueror.

Lil was at the door to greet him. But she saw his face.

"What's wrong?"

"Let me inside."

...

The jeans were cut, so he only winced a little when they extended the tear all the way down to the cuff to expose the wound. At home, it would be a quick visit to Lewistown Clinic for a couple of stitches and a round of antibiotics. Here, it was a little more serious. Speaker Joseph directed Samuel. They bathed the cut in spring water and brought in the brazier.

Lil whispered, "I have a first aid kit, but it's at the copper room. I'm so sorry I forgot to bring it."

"It's okay. We're leaving soon."

Speaker Joseph asked, "Are you ready?"

He nodded. Lil averted her eyes while the Speaker applied the glowing metal poker to sear the flesh. Samuel watched every move and asked questions. Every instinct told him to escape the searing metal. He nearly sprained his fingers, gripping the bench to hold himself still.

Lil applied a cotton compress and put a couple of stitches in the pants leg to keep it from flapping. The pain was only fading slowly. The cure was much worse than the cut.

She objected when he declared his intent to go back down the hill. "Those burns are not stitches and my cotton isn't secured. It will do no good to go down there and have your wound break open again. And I will not have you come down with a septic infection, not in this place."

He relented. They sat together on the observation rock where he could watch the progress. The levee breech was filled and the towns-folk gathered to share out the trade goods. He couldn't wish that task on anyone, but Terry and Wilson seemed to have everything well in hand. Several times, the housewives would come up on the hill and thank Lady Lillian profusely for the fancy cloth, or the bone buttons, or the needles, or the tin of seeds that seemed to be more than their wildest fancy could imagine. None of them thanked him, although he suspected it was a cultural thing. None of the women had ever talked to him directly, other than that first sentence when the lady thought Lil was sick.

He watched the raiders build a much smaller raft from the broken pieces of their original. Terry came up and asked if he wanted any final words with them.

"No. I said what I wanted. It's your town, you can add anything else you want."

Terry went back down. Jerry stood, visible on the overlook, although it was painful. He wanted to be seen whole and hearty.

The raiders piled onto the small raft, including the injured. Jerry suspected that the man with the shattered leg and the two with sword injuries might not make it. He said nothing, although he ached to follow his 'Modern American' instincts and provide care for the wounded.

But this was not his age. This was not his home. He kept his shame hidden.

Terry had his say, and then the men poled away from shore. Soon, they were out of sight. Jerry looked upriver. Soon enough more would come.

. . .

Lil wanted to leave, to get back to her first aid kit with its topical antibiotics and its sterile bandages, and if necessary, a jump through time to a hospital. But he had things to say first.

The two young men that the town had designated as blacksmith trainees showed up, carrying the sword he'd knocked from the raider's hand. Like it was an enchanted thing, they presented it to him.

He swung it through the air and felt its balance. It was so much better than the crude sword he'd held. The blade was sharp and the grip was bone or something like that, with a regular guard to protect the hand. He pointed out the features to Seth and Lenid, ages 12 and 14.

"When you can make a blade as fine as this, only then can you call yourselves master blacksmiths. Now take it. Keep the blade oiled and free of rust. You will have more to make than swords, but I want you to pull this out from time to time and study it. Make me proud." They were wide eyed, and had no words. He showed them out when Terry, Wilson and a couple of others came in.

...

"We would like you to stay with us."

Across the room, Lil was watching and he could see her strain to overhear. She wanted to come join him, but this was a men's council and she was well aware of the conventions.

He nodded. "I have felt the desire to stay, but I have other obligations, and our journey is far from over."

Wilson spread out his hands. "You have defeated the slavers, but there will be more."

"No. You defeated them. You and the river. You dug the channel and prepared the levee. I am just a stranger passing through. It was your skills and your bravery that won the battle."

"But we can't flood the town every time a barge comes by."

Jerry leaned forward to make his point, "Which is why you need to build the barricade across the lock as I said. You have materials at hand from the remainder of the barge."

He held up one finger. "If they try to come through the lock and are blocked, then their barge is just as stranded as if it were stuck in Wilson's muddy field. They would have to crawl across the barricade if they wanted to fight, and they would be helpless against your defense."

He held up a second. "If a raider comes before you get the barricade built, then raise the white flag and sell them the bags of grain you salvaged from the first barge."

And a third, "But make this point. Drag the wreckage of the barge up onto the levee where they can see it at a distance and keep a fire burning near the flag—you have plenty of wood.

"Your ancestors built the dam long, long ago to tame the river, and it's your inheritance. You own this part of the river. You can make the water flow where you will, and the barge men know that, deep in their guts.

"You will have to destroy another barge, and it will take at least another season before they have all heard the story. Even then, some will want to test you. But if you hold them off, and yet trade fairly under the white flag, then the law of the river will have changed forever."

...

When they were gone, and Lil pulled him under the blanket, she whispered, "You could have stayed. They'd have made you their king."

"Only until I made my first huge mistake and got someone killed. No. I'm no prince in disguise. I just want to get out of here before they figure out what a fraud I've been."

"You didn't look like a fraud to me. You fought the bad guys and rescued the slaves and brought some real hope to a town that lived in fear."

He shook his head. "Who knows what the results will be? No change like this comes without a cost. Which is best, to live a simple life and stay free as long as you can run fast, or to fight to change the status quo, to gain some pride and lose some innocence?"

"Oh, just go to sleep, Jeremy Harris."

"Oof"

"What?"

"You just put some pressure on my leg."

"Sorry. Now go to sleep."

. . .

The morning was bright and Jerry slept past dawn for the first time. The word had gone out. They were leaving. Everyone wanted to say goodbye. A good number wanted them to stay.

Jerry looked at the number of women who clustered around Lil. He smiled. He'd been worried she wouldn't be able to cope in a place where the genders were so separated, but he shouldn't have. She'd been deeply involved the whole time, and he was much more isolated from the women's world than she was from the men's matters.

A big share of the captured trade goods were reserved for them, and Lil took a practical look at them and added a couple of items to her travel bag, but for the most part, they gave it back to the town.

"We will have to travel light. You understand. We need to be on our way. Goodbye."

Lil whispered in his ear.

Jerry turned to the Speaker and the men and said, "Lady Lillian would like to speak to everyone?" There was no objection.

Lil took a step forward. The crowd grew quiet.

"In some ways, when I came here I was lost. I have lost my family and I may never see them again in this life. But you have been a family to me. We have shared together, sung together, and prayed together. You have filled part of my heart that was empty. I will never forget you."

. . .

Terry offered to send a couple of the older boys along part of the way, just to look out for dangers on the way, but Jerry declined. "We have to go alone."

He whispered to Lil, "Wave, and then don't look back."

They were a quarter mile back towards the copper room when he glanced around and was confident that they were not being followed. In the space of a hundred steps, he sagged and began limping.

"Are you okay?"

"The leg hurts. The burn is excruciating every step. I had to hide it when they were looking."

"Silly man. Do you want to take a rest? Find a place to sit?"

"No. Someone will take it into their head to follow. We need to be sealed up and gone."

They made the rest of the trip at a fast hobble.

. . .

Lil said, "Sit on the bed, but don't get under the sheets—not until we get you cleaned up."

He relaxed with a sigh.

"Is the door latched?"

"Yes. Now unzip your jeans."

"Lil!" He grinned, thinly.

"Don't get any ideas. I need to check your leg."

Together they got them free. She tossed him the towel. "These stink. Cover up with this and take it all off. I have to get them washed." She turned her back.

"Okay."

He was stretched out on the bed and strategically covered. She pulled a chair close and began unwrapping the cotton from the seeping wound.

"I'll have to treat this again. It re-opened."

He nodded. He had felt it happen.

The first aid kit was designed for smaller wounds, but she was liberal with the antibacterial and antifungal ointments after swabbing with alcohol. She could hear his teeth grinding as she worked.

"I'm going to use some of your precious battery power to run the microwave for a couple of minutes."

"Why?"

"I'm going to sterilize a needle and thread and stitch the wound."

"Do you know how?"

"Summer camp for years. I worked with the counselors and we had our share of injuries. I held a few hands as the little ones got treated. I've never done it myself, but I watched."

He nodded. "Good."

She plugged the microwave in and put the thread and needle in a cup covered in an inch of water. She nuked it on high until the water boiled away. She dabbed her fingers in alcohol and carried the cup over to the bed.

"Try not to jerk."

It was nearly impossible to make that first needle insertion. She felt the needle go in and imagined the pain herself.

I'm just stuffing a turkey, binding it back together.

He grunted, and she hurried. *I hope I remember the stitching pattern.* She looped the thread each stitch and tied the final knot. The ugly burns made it all the more difficult.

"You're going to scar."

He shrugged.

When she was done, she re-sterilized the area and bound it with gauze.

"That will have to do."

He nodded. She frowned.

"Are you okay?"

"As well as can be expected. Are we ready to move on?"

"No. As long as we have a this relatively secluded hideout. I want to wash your clothes. I'm sure the sheep won't mind me stealing some of their water."

"We don't want to be caught, or discovered."

"I know. You just rest for now."

Lil went to the door and opened it a crack. Other than the placid red sheep, there was no sign of any movement.

As soon as she stepped outside, with her white dress swirling around her legs, she had second thoughts and went back inside.

Anyone could see me for miles in this dress.

Jerry had begun to snore. It disturbed her. Had his injury taken more of a toll than she was aware? If he had an infection, he might have a fever. She'd have to monitor him.

She unpacked her cheerleader outfit. It was hardly modest for the era, but the reds were much better camouflage than white.

She checked Jerry again, but he really looked asleep. Quietly, she changed clothes.

This time, she slipped past the sheep and peered through the gate. There were trees less that fifty feet away, and in her own time, to the left of the woods was a little pond. Could it still be there? The water for the sheep had to come from somewhere.

That was a thought. Every few days the shepherd had to bring water to this pen and fill the trough. He'd leave a track.

And sure enough, there was a footpath that veered off to the left of the line of trees.

Am I great or what! So, should she bring water here, or carry the dirty clothes to the water?

I'm only going in the night, regardless of what color clothes I wear.

But that could be arranged.

She packed the dirty clothes in a bag. Stinky! Then she checked the dial carefully. 3600X was one hour per second. She set it and flipped the switch, counting to ten. And then off.

Outside it was night time, with just a hint of moonlight. Perfect. She crept out, looking for any signs of people.

The path was barely visible. She carried her cell phone for light, but if she never used it, that would be best. It would be hard to explain.

About five hundred feet down the edge of the woods, she saw a light, the flicker of a campfire. The shepherd's camp, she suspected. Circling it widely, she nearly stumbled into the creek. She tried to match her memories with this landscape and failed. Perhaps the pond was gone, but the water still flowed. That was enough for her.

With moonlight filtering in through the overhead branches, she found a pool big enough to work with. She took off her shoes and began scrubbing Jerry's clothes, using just brute force and spring water.

She missed soap. She should have picked some up in the village, but there had been so much going on, she didn't think about it.

There was a noise in the underbrush and she froze. There it was again. There! A boy was walking along a path, swinging at the bushes with a stick. He was maybe eight. Was he out here alone?

She kept an eye on him as she worked on the clothes, wringing as much water as she could from the soggy fabric. Through a gap in the trees, she saw him hang up his cap, put one last log on the fire, and burrow under his blankets.

I guess they start them young out here.

She put her shoes back on, and gathered the laundry. Careful to make as little sound as possible, she crept back towards the copper room.

Inside, she draped the wet clothes across the backs of the chairs.

I've got to unload my phone, and recharge it. It looked as if it were going to flicker and go dead any second. Good thing she hadn't needed it as a flashlight.

During their short stay, she'd managed to record six hours of audio, enough video for a couple of youtubes and an unknown number of photos. She didn't have much hope for the photos. Lots of those were at odd angles, as she hid the phone from sight.

As the files moved through the wires, she heard a drip, drip, drip. There was a puddle below the wet clothes, and a lifetime of training couldn't bear the thought of ruining the finish on the wooden chairs either.

Okay, I need to hang them outside to dry.

Lil was a girl of her time and had always used a tumble dryer, but her grandmother had a clothes line constructed like a big beach umbrella in her back yard, so she was aware of the process.

I'll need the sun. If she could arrange night, she could arrange daylight. She flipped the switch a couple of times and checked outside. She circled the area inside the stone fence, looking for a good place to hang them.

The gate through the outer walls faced north, as had the house before it had burned down, but the copper room faced west. The south side was the perfect place for the laundry, hidden from the entrance gate. If the shepherd boy only entered to drop off hay or fill the water trough, he might never see anything out of the ordinary.

Unfortunately, as she looked around the long decayed piles of rubble, the remnants of the collapsed walls, she didn't see anything she could use as a clothesline. Not even grass grew inside the enclosure—or if it did, it didn't survive the sheep.

She'd need something from the woods, like a branch or something.

A pair of sheep eyes locked with hers.

A long branch. Something that would keep Jerry's jeans from becoming someone's lunch.

But crossing over into the woods would be best in darkness. She smiled. *I can do that.*

Door. Dial. Switch. And it was dark.

There was moonlight enough. She rummaged through the bushes, grumbling that although she had four outfits now, the gym shorts and top, the cheerleader outfit, the regular shirt and blouse she wore to school that day, and her new long white dress, what she really needed for tramping through the woods was a pair of long pants. Something was biting at her legs.

She found the perfect branch, long and L-shaped. It was twice as tall as she was. She switched back to daylight and draped Jerry's clothes on them, then pushed it up against the south wall of the room. Jumping a few more hours to evening, she retrieved them before risk of dew. They were dry and smelling clean. The whole process took her less subjective time than using a tumble dryer. It would have been much less if she hadn't had to find a clothes line.

She was barely back inside, when there sounded a tap on the door, from the outside! Someone had seen her. Panicked, she latched the doorway, dialed the time shift to a high setting and flipped the switch on and off.

Several years at least. She smiled. It was great to be able to outrun your mistakes like that.

Year 406

As she was humming to herself as she put a tighter set of stitches in the torn jeans some time later, Jerry muttered, "Hi."

"Oh, sorry. Did I wake you?"

"No."

She sat on the bed and checked his leg. "How are you feeling?"

He shrugged. "Tired."

"I've got your clothes cleaned and dried."

He nodded, not much cheered. She'd have liked to brag about all she'd done, but he just seemed down. Last night, he'd said something about being a fraud. Was he still down about what he'd done?

"Cheer up. You saved the day, protected the village, and even won a sword fight. Pretty good deal."

He shook his head. "I lost that sword fight. It was pure accident I came out alive." He shifted his leg. "I'm the one that came away injured. He just fell down."

"He was the one who had his hands tied in the end. Sounds like a win to me. Now," she sniffed and wrinkled her nose, "I've got your clothes clean, but you still smell."

He shifted in the bed. "I'll clean up..."

"No. You stay put. Your cut needs to heal and you may have a slight infection. I want you to stay put and rest. I'll get some water and wash you myself."

He smiled. But it was too weak a reaction for her taste. What kind of a guy wouldn't be trilled to get a sponge bath from a cheerleader? He had to be feeling a reaction from the injury.

She made sure he stretched out again, and then went to the door. Outside, it was dark.

A full moon made it easy to confirm that the water trough was gone. The gate to the walled-in pen was wide open and didn't appear used.

What was she going to use for water? Was there anything inside the copper room she could use? Coke cans or something?

Something was stacked up against the far stone wall. It was a shepherd's staff, a leather bucket, and a wooden box. She peered inside with the help of her cell phone light. It looked like a knife, a pair of shears, and a couple of stones. Just tools.

But the bucket was just what she needed. She made the crossing over to the woods again, following the path to the creek. Just as before, she saw the flicker of light from the campsite and smelled woodsmoke faintly on the breeze.

Moving slowly and trying not to make any noise, she veered away from the campsite to where she remembered the pool in the creek.

It was already occupied.

My, how you've grown.

The shepherd was nearer her age now, bathing in the creek.

Frozen, trying not to breathe, she backed her way out. Glad no one could see her blushes in the dark, she moved a hundred yards upstream and quietly filled her bucket. As soon as she was clear, she hurried just as fast as she could move back to the copper room. She arrived huffing and puffing.

She closed the door and latched it.

"Are you okay?"

"Sure. It's just a long walk from the creek."

Lil set the bucket down by the bed. She had the water, it was time to start.

"I'm going to need the towel. Use the edge of the blanket," she ordered and turned her back. Eyes averted, she tugged the towel free. He shifted his position.

She turned back and smiled. "Okay, I'm going to start at the top." She wet the corner of the towel and began washing his face, then drying with the other end.

He appeared to be enjoying it, by the time she'd finished his neck and began working on his arms, a smile crept onto his face.

She rinsed the mud from the towel and began on his chest. The smile was larger.

"You appear to be having a good time." She was happy to see it. Seeing him step up be a leader had been impressive, but what had attracted her from the beginning was his smile and sense of humor.

"Mmm."

"Does that feel good?"

"Yes. Even better if we swapped."

Confusion at what he meant only lasted a fraction of a second. That flash of image hit her like slipping into a hot tub. Heat spread all through her. Her hands shook a little, uncertain which way to move.

"Lil?"

"Ah. Right." She hurried up, washing his torso, the strokes more brisk and businesslike than before. She rinsed the wet side of the towel again. "You need to handle the next zone." She turned her back, the chair scraping on the floor.

He made noises. Just ordinary noises as he shifted around and scrubbed. The sounds of his body were deafening. She could feel him, across the gap of a foot or so, right there behind her.

Her face was burning. She could feel it out to the tips of her ears.

How much of their flirtation had been real? They smiled, they kissed, and it was all so perfect. These past few days, 'pretending', being so close together, sleeping in the same bed together—she loved it.

But he'd set guidelines, and so had she. It was all pretend, wasn't it?

Before their time shift, they'd played out that slow dating dance, getting to know each other, seeing what little intimacies they could steal out of sight of her parents. Nothing had been set in stone. Their calendar had stretched out to sometime in the summer, when college would drag them away. She'd played with ideas where she'd change schools, or he would.

It was different now, wasn't it? Maybe it wasn't pretend. But was it real for him?

Guys thought about girls and sex differently, didn't they?

"I'm decent now."

She turned back and took the towel, rinsing it again.

Breathe slowly. Don't get carried away. Don't let him see me flustered. She concentrated on his mud-streaked legs, getting them back to their proper color.

"I'm not ever going to let you play in the mud again."

"Okay." He put his arms behind his head and let her work. He seemed at ease. That...explosion...of heat that had nearly knocked her over must not have happened for him.

And it wasn't over for her. She hurried to the end.

"This rinse water is vile. I'm going to throw it out." She hurried for the door and was outside as quickly as she was able. She emptied the bucket and carried it back to the shepherd's stash of tools.

The box caught her attention again. She opened it and picked up the shears. Jerry should see these.

He looked up when she came back in and turned on another light. "Look at these."

Jerry worked the blades and examined the u-shaped spring that held it all together.

"This is iron. Where did you find it?"

"I jumped maybe a decade or so ahead in time as I kept going out, doing chores. I didn't want to be seen."

She didn't mention the tapping on the door.

"So, our blacksmiths could have made it locally."

"Or gotten it in trade."

He nodded. "Either one is a good sign. Better put it back. It's probably valuable."

She went back out, and put the shears in the box. The cool night air was welcome, so she walked slowly, taking time to peer out at the woods.

Have to be careful there too. I'm surrounded by naked sexy men.

She went back in, latching the door.

He watched her. "I'm feeling better now. And I'm under the sheets. Feels better than the blanket."

Every word he said had dangerous extra meanings for her. And even covered from the waist down, he looked too good.

He patted the bed beside him. She sat as if she had no will of her own.

"It sounds like you've been busy. What have you been up to while I was asleep?"

"Oh, this and that. I washed and dried your clothes." Her adventure spanning years, with all her clever planning and execution—over in six words. His hand rested on her knee and it was all she could think about.

Cleaned up, and chipper, he looked and smelled so good. "You look better."

He moved his hand a few inches up her leg. "You look great. I've alway loved the cheerleader look."

"Ah." She couldn't breathe. "I need..."

"What?" His eyes were clear and honest and pulled at her.

She swallowed. "I think I need to take a walk...outside. It's a little warm in here." She got to her feet.

"Oh, we can just open the door for a while. I have the air system turned off to save battery." He reached for the sheet. "I'll just..."

She moved to the door. "You need to rest. Just. Stay. Heal."

He chuckled. "You make me sound like a dog."

And I'm a bitch in heat. She set the dial and pushed them twenty years along.

"You're getting pretty familiar with that."

She went out the door. "I'll be back in a bit."

As soon as he could no longer see her, she dashed for the open gateway and into the night.

Year 426

It was another moon-lit night, but clouds were hurrying across the sky. Weather was coming, but it wasn't here yet. It was reckless of her to be out now, with no reason other than to get some control over herself. It was cool, and she needed to run.

The road to town had a few more trees in it than she remembered, but there was also a worn path that she hadn't seen before. Was that from the shepherd or was this, like it had been in her day, a route into town from other places?

No answers tonight. Just questions. She headed towards the river.

She kept pace long enough to get a glimpse of the town. Being seen, especially dressed as she was, would be a big mistake.

Whoa. She wished she had her phone to take a picture, but in this light, it probably wouldn't show anything anyway. *Jerry should see the changes.* The two barges docked alongside a much expanded waterfront under a white flag said a lot. More than double the houses, the town was packed more densely, and the church was larger and whitewashed.

No more. She had to get back before her impulsiveness could turn catastrophic.

She walked back, keeping to the edge of the trees so even the faint moonlight wouldn't betray her.

The sheep objected. A large flock, mixed red and white, with an occasional black one showed why they weren't using the stone pen anymore. The red variety had multiplied and no longer needed special protection.

I wonder what happened to my little shepherd boy?

Her heartbeat had calmed. The jittery hands and the burning inside her had subsided. A good night's sleep—not in the same bed with Jerry—would put everything back to right. How she would manage that, she didn't know, but she'd deal with it after a quick peek into the woods.

The creek was still there, but the shepherd's camp had changed. There was now a little hut, hardly larger than her walk-in closet back home. No one was there and the campfire was just banked coals. With the flickering moonlight, as little clouds drifted by, she risked a closer look.

The hut had a bed, and a familiar wooden box, probably with the same tools inside. She was tempted to take a peek, but she needed to be able to dash for safety.

No sooner had she thought about it, than she heard steps. Footsteps and a thud, and it was coming from her escape direction. The darkness hid any other exits. She ducked behind the hut, and found a protected little spot in the trees. If he went inside, she might be able to tiptoe past in the dark.

A gruff-looking man with a staff walked into the camp. He sat heavily on a bench made from a large log. He tossed some wood on the coals and blew at them. A little trickle of yellow appeared, very bright compared to the filtered moonlight. She tried to stay hidden.

In less than a minute, he had the fire going well. By the yellow light, she saw that he was missing his right arm from the elbow. He stared at the flickering light, and said, "Lady in the trees, I'm glad you're back."

She was frozen in place. Had he seen her, or was it just some rambling thought?

"Come over to the fire. I'll make you a place." He vacated the log bench and sat down a few feet to the other side.

I can probably run faster than he can. But she was trapped where she was.

She wanted Jerry so badly.

Collecting herself, she slipped between the tree trunks and sat at the bench, trying to sit as modestly as possible in a cheerleader's short skirt.

"Hello."

He grinned widely. "Knew you were real. I knew it from the first time I saw you, when I was little."

He stirred the fire and added another log. "My Pa said it was nonsense, I was just scared of the woods. But there were little things. There were tracks, lady tracks, where there shouldn't be. My tools and stuff moved. I knew it. Green Lady of the Trees, barely there at all, watching out for me. Saw you twice, for sure. Just hints other times."

He shook his head. "My brothers taught me quick not to say anything." He rubbed his head.

So, she was a tree nymph, or something. She was touched that he thought she was his guardian angel. She'd done nothing for him.

"I'm sorry for your arm."

He raised the stump and looked at it. "Old story. My fault. Shoulda never got into the war."

War? Would asking about it jinx the idea she was supernatural? And maybe she didn't want to know. It was probably not something she should tell Jerry, not until a few hundred years had passed.

His voice went lower, "I know why you are here now."

"Oh?"

"Is Death comin' tonight?"

"No. No, it's not."

He sighed. "I know it won't be too long. I know as well as anyone what that lump in my belly means. My granddad had the same thing. No help for it."

She could see tears in his eyes, sparkling in the firelight. She could feel them in her eyes as well.

What a world! Back home, cancer meant endless medical treatments and words of hope and hours and hours on the Internet, trying to understand which variety responded to which chemo and what the doctors' words meant.

Here it was simple. A death sentence.

And there was nothing she could do about it.

He saw her eyes. "Don't fret over me. I'd a good life. A special one." He meant her.

He stirred the fire, pushing the wood together for a brighter, if briefer, flame. They sat in silence for a moment.

If I could do something for him... But there was nothing. Having grown up with elaborate medical options didn't mean she had them in her blood. Those were gone with the dust.

A cough and a look in his downcast eyes meant there was something on his mind.

"Tell me. What are you thinking about?" she asked.

He shifted his position. "It's not my place to ask."

Oh no, if he asks to be healed what will I say?

As gently as she could, she whispered, "I won't be offended."

He sighed. "It's just. My little boy. Cal. He'll be taking my staff in a few days. Sally made me promise I'd stay to home. Up here, it can be a hard life. So quiet my Pa wasn't at all surprised I'd imagined you. I worry about him.

"Would it be...possible for you to look over him?"

She bit off the impulse to promise her shepherd boy anything. It might be comforting, but it would be a lie.

"I'm...limited. I couldn't be there for you in your war. I can't promise all that you might want for him."

He nodded. "I understand. But would you?"

She prayed for just the right word. Just the right comfort to say.

And then she had a thought.

"Have you spoken to the Speaker?"

"Speaker Stephen?" He looked embarrassed. "I been to church a few times. Just a few. The sheep don't care about Sundays."

"Okay, I will make you a deal. Listen carefully."

He leaned forward.

"You need to go talk to Speaker Stephen. Tell him to teach you Psalms 23, word for word, until you can say it yourself. And then you need to teach your boy Cal to say it word for word. Can you do that?"

He looked worried. "Speaker Stephen is an important man. I don't know if he'll have time to talk to someone like me."

She stood up. "Then you say these words to Speaker Stephen. 'You promised a lady a favor, in exchange for the little book. Now she asks this favor of you.'"

His mouth was working, as if he were repeating the words to himself, memorizing them.

She added, "If you will do this: Teach young Cal the words of Psalms 23 from your own mouth, then I will look over him."

He stumbled to his feet. "I'll do it. I'll do it. But...but I know of the little book! The Speaker has told the story, of how Lady Lillian handed it to him for the blessing of the town on the day she left. Does that mean that you are...Lady Lillian?"

She stood silent. Her brain raced for something to say.

Her shepherd nodded. "Okay. I know some things are not meant to be known. But please...does that mean Lord Jeremy is like you?"

Oh, what have I gotten myself into! There was nothing she could tell him. And the story of timeless ones could be very harmful if it got out.

She reached out and took his hand. It was very rough and dry. And how old was he? Forty-ish. And due to die shortly.

"Some things must not be told. You understand?"

He nodded vigorously.

"Okay. I can only tell you this. He is nearby, resting."

He strained to hear more, but that was all she would tell him.

He nodded and bowed to her. "Thank you. Thank you. Thank you."

Before he had said it twice, she had made her dash to escape, running just as hard as she could, wishing with all her heart that he wouldn't try to follow.

...

Jerry was fully dressed and reading at the table when she came in, breathless.

"You are out of bed!" she accused.

"You told me to rest and heal. I took an extra day, in short jumps so I wouldn't have to use the air system. The cut is much better now. It itches like crazy, but there's no infection. I ...."

"Tell me later. I need your help right now. We need to jump exactly one year into the future. Help me get the settings right."

"What?"

"I'll explain later. It's something I have to do. Help me."

He used the calculator and the 250,000X calibrated setting to jump them close. She looked out the door and checked the angle of the sun. "Another eight hours. I need the darkness."

They made the correction.

"I should go with you."

She shook her head firmly. "Absolutely not. This is dangerous enough as it is. If I'm not back in thirty minutes, then you can come looking for me, but not before!"

"I wish you would tell me what's going on."

"Maybe I will. Later. But this is important to me. Understand?"

He nodded. "Okay, but the stopwatch is running. Be safe."

Year 427

She hurried out into the night, taking extra care. It was an overcast, moonless night.

But the fire was lit and a little boy was cooking something shapeless, toasting it over the flames. She waited a few minutes in her hiding place, conscious of her deadline. But the moment had to be right. He set his stick aside and took a sip from a skin at his feet.

In a loud voice, she said, "Cal. You look just like your father did."

He was up on his feet, mouth open. He looked around, but didn't see her.

"Lady? Lady is that you?"

She waited until he ducked into the hut, looking even there, and made her escape.

It was a stupid, reckless, risk. But maybe one more shepherd would think he had a special life.

...

Jerry was able to breathe a sigh of relief when she appeared in the gateway. He'd been waiting in the darkness. She hadn't made a sound as she approached.

He gave her a hug. "Come on in."

She sat down, looking drained.

"Did it go okay?"

She nodded. "Perfectly."

"Would you like something to eat?"

"A little something. It's been a long day for me. I need to sleep."

He stretched his memory. It had been nearly two days since he'd left town, but had Lil gotten any sleep since then? Was it still the same day for her?

"Certainly. The bed's all yours. I'll be reading for a few hours yet." He reached into the satchel and handed her the last of the Regat's food. She munched on it silently.

"You'll tell me all the gory details?"

She nodded. "But tomorrow."

"Should we put some days behind us?"

"Might as well. At least a few years or so."

He nodded and shifted them twenty.

Year 447

Opening the door a crack, he saw it was daylight. "I might read outside, if that's okay? I'm feeling a little cooped up."

"Fine. I need to change anyway."

He smiled, "I could help."

That'd usually get a sly response, but she was clearly too tired. She just shook her head.

He took his classic history book, *The Face of Battle*, and a bottle of water and went outside, closing the door behind him. A careful check of the surroundings showed a lot of red sheep and not much else. There was a large stone that he hadn't seen before. It was positioned against the inside west wall and made a perfect bench. Perhaps the shepherds used it for something. In any case, it made a comfortable place to sit and read while keeping an eye on both the copper room's door and the outside.

He'd been hitting the books heavily since Lil had started acting mysterious. Not that he expected any answers to the way girls work, but just as a way to break free of the worries that had been circling in his head like vultures over a dead cow. He was grateful for his bag of books and the impulse to make the most of the 'study room' while he had access to unlimited time.

Overdue library books were now one more crime on his ledger—but probably those libraries had gone the way of Alexandria.

The sun was near noon, and maybe a little too bright for reading. It would get better shortly when the high stone wall's shadow covered the bench. He dismissed the impulse to move the sun for reading convenience. He'd just wait on it. The batteries were still greater than 50%, even after all those waiting times he took while she was out on her walk. Before too long he'd need to either find, or invent, electricity. Somewhere in his books was probably a diagram of a generator, but it might take years to work out the differences between an idealized science illustration and a workable generator—at least one that worked well enough to charge the batteries.

And he was worried about Lil.

The memory of her leaning over his body, washing him, her cute uniform bringing back so many earlier fantasies—something had happened then. She'd retreated. Had he done something then? Or was it a reaction to their unique exile?

Somehow, he'd expected shouts and tears and anger. What he'd done to her was equivalent to kidnapping. She'd lost her home and family more certainly than if they'd all been killed. Her folks had died, one way or another, and from her point of view, it must have been as shocking and abrupt as a car accident.

Was it just delayed shock? What's more important, would she get over it?

He didn't know, but with her changes—her non-response to his teasing and her mysterious outside activities, giving her some space was probably the best course. It would be easy enough to keep on different sleeping schedules for now. He could avoid crowding her, avoid touching her, avoid trying to sleep next to her, until things got better.

He shook his head. It wasn't his first choice. Sharing the bed had been the high point of their exile, at least for him.

When he started re-living the sword fight in his head, again, he picked up the book. He had to shake this pattern of these repeating worries.

He found his bookmark and forced his attention back to 1415 and the Battle of Agincourt.

...

It was mid-afternoon when a muffled thud caught his attention. He looked at the metal door, still closed. He'd opened it every forty-five minutes, just to make sure the air was freshened, and to take a peek at sleeping Lil. She was a tempting sight in her gym outfit, curled up under the sheets. Not tempting enough to go back on his good intentions, but enough that he lingered at the door, watching her breathe.

But a second sound told him it hadn't come from within the copper room. Before he could react, a man walked through the stone entranceway, dressed in a dust-covered coat and slacks, carrying an artist's easel.

"Whoa. Thua startled me there."

Jerry nodded. He had to play it out. The iron door was closed, but not latched, and he didn't know if the conversation would penetrate enough to wake Lil.

"Sorry. I wasn't expecting you either."

The man propped his easel against the wall and held out his hand. "Apprentice Journeler Meade."

"Harris. Uh...Jay Harris." They shook.

"Are you local, Mr. Harris? Or a scholar checking out the artifact?"

"Artifact?"

Meade smiled. He nodded toward the copper room. "That's my take. But you're a scholar, right. With the clothes and the book, I'd hardly expect you to be a sheep rancher."

Jerry nodded. "You're right. I'm a student. Although, I wasn't studying the artifact. The bench was just a nice place to sit and read. What do you know about it?"

Mead unfolded his easel and placed his drawing board on it. "You haven't heard of it? The locals think it's some kind of religious shrine. They call it the 'Doorway to Heaven'. Personally, what with the reddish walls and the black door, I'd call it the 'Doorway to Hell'."

Jerry looked at it critically. "Looks like a copper box to me."

Meade was sketching out the rough lines. "You'd think so, wouldn't you? But the fact is some miners came by here about ten years ago, wanting to buy it and melt it down. But the problem was that they couldn't scratch the surface, not with a drill or an axe or anything. Of course, the locals nearly hung them for trying.

"So, it looks like copper, but it's stronger than any known metal. That makes it an artifact. And I know artifacts!"

"Oh?"

He beamed. "I'm from St. Louis University. That city has lots of artifacts, and once you've seen the Fallen Arch up close, it's hard to be impressed by them—much less make them into holy shrines."

He began applying shading to his sketch. "Still. You can scratch the Fallen Arch—there must be a thousand names scratched into it. And that door handle there is so tempting. Everybody who sees it tries to open it. I had a go at it myself yesterday.

"Of course the locals have a legend for that as well."

"Tell me. I didn't know this place was so fascinating."

"Yep. The story is right out of King Arthur. You know the story of Canton—everybody does. Upstart farming town that took to block-ading the river traffic and confiscating the goods. They rebuilt the old dam and control the gate. Well the Lake Country took offense and there was quite a little border war in these parts. Well it got resolved. Treaty of Canton and all that. Everybody's happy. Major shipping center now, although nothing like the Sloo, of course."

Jerry's grip on his history book likely left indents. It took all his resolve to keep the sick feeling in his stomach from showing on his face.

War, and I caused it.

But Meade wasn't done.

"So the way the locals tell it, their rise to prominence came when a Lord somebody came through town and taught them how to fight, how to work iron, how to likely read and write from the way they tell it. And the thing is, he did it all in one day, captured the first barge single-handed and fought a duel to the death with the captain. Then he walked away and was never heard from again."

He was gesturing more in his storytelling with his brush than he was using it making his drawing.

"But another version says that this Lord and his Lady were angels in disguise—that's where the 'Doorway to Heaven' comes from—and another version of the tale is that Lord whoever is sleeping in some nearby cave and will return to rescue Canton in the hour of its greatest need. Or that when his successor arrives, he'll be able to open the door when no one else can."

Jerry took another breath. "Where do people come up with these stories?"

Meade shook his head. "But you can see why I was commissioned to paint this place. Artifact or holy shrine, it's a great story and the King loves to brag about the Western Shore. Lake Country has been too superior for too long. That's why our King aided Canton, even though it was hurting Sloo's commerce as well."

While Meade was turned his way, Jerry thought he saw the door open a crack and then silently close.

Lil, keep it shut. Jump a day if you have to. This chatterbox can't see it open.

Jerry stood up and moved over closer to the painting, where he could see it better. Meade shifted his stance so he could keep his audience in view.

"You're a tall one. You know they say their mystical Lord fellow was a giant, too."

Jerry chuckled. He pointed at the copper room.

"What do you think this artifact does?"

The painter frowned. "I'm not one to say. There's a lot of speculation about what Golden Age science was capable of doing—flying through the air, talking great distances, even visiting the stars. Who can say what they might have left behind?"

Jerry sounded skeptical. "You believe all that stuff?"

Meade nodded. "I had my doubts growing up, like everyone else, but once you've been in the Hall of Records and seen videos—it's hard to remain skeptical."

"Videos. Are those something common in Sloo?"

"Oh no. Scholars only. But if you can wrangle an invitation, it's worth your while to see it. The Librarians make you wear a white robe, for cleanliness, they say. You walk into a little room and stare at a blank wall. An apprentice starts cranking a large handle, and pictures, moving pictures, appear on the wall."

His voice lowered, and he stared Jerry straight in the eye. "And those pictures were from the Golden Age itself!" He shook his head. "I just can't describe what I saw."

Jerry thought it was unlikely that Meade could be struck dumb, but he didn't say much else for a few minutes. He concentrated on his painting.

With nothing better to do himself, Jerry took a close look at the copper room. He'd help build it, but from this perspective, everything looked different. Uncle Greg and he had hung heavy sheets of copper directly onto the studs, and Greg had welded the seams together himself. The floor and ceiling had been done with a heavier grade of copper, but the walls had been much thinner.

The room before him should have been held together by metal studs on the outside, but there was no sign of them. If he remembered the weight of those sheets, if the studs had fallen away or corroded, the heavy ceiling should have begun to crumple the walls by its very weight.

He moved closer to the door opening. Yes, the walls had been made thicker than he remembered.

"See something interesting?" asked Meade.

"Oh, I'm just looking at the thickness of the walls."

"Yes. I read the miner's report before I came. They said it appeared to be two layers thick. You should be able to see where the layers meet in the doorway."

And there it was. A second, much layer of copper had been added, and from what he remembered putting the first layer in place, that would have nearly been impossible, not without tearing down the outer plaster walls and moving new sheets in place.

Which is what Uncle Greg must have done. But why?

Only one idea came to the surface. The copper room wasn't safe as a stand-alone structure. *Uncle Greg did it to protect Lil and me.* The house and its supporting studs wouldn't last forever. If they had come out of time stasis without the surrounding house, the room would have immediately collapsed on them. So he had built it stronger.

"You say the miners couldn't scratch the surface?"

"That's right. You can try it yourself. I tried. No luck."

"I believe you."

But that meant that the protection of slowed time must have extended out to include the new copper layers. But it looked corroded like an old penny.

Had the time effects crept out over time, or had it only been included only after they stopped moving in time and restarted? Puzzles to think about when they weren't in danger of being discovered.

"How long does it take to paint your picture?"

"Oh, I'll have the rough image done before the sunlight fades, but I'll probably have to come back for a week or so, to get the details perfect."

Jerry talked a little louder, facing the door. "Yes, I guess you can't do too much here without sunlight."

"No, and I'd like to be headed back to the inn in town before it gets too dark. This road doesn't see a lot of carts. Every time the wheel hit a stone, I feared for my paints."

"Hey! Did you see that?"

"See what?" Jerry had seen it, but feigned ignorance. There had been a slight change in color. Lil had taken the hint and jumped ahead.

Meade frowned at the copper room. "I guess it was a cloud layer moving by or something. The light changed suddenly."

"Well, you're the painter. I guess I'd better get back to my book while I have the light myself."

...

Meade could not help himself, he chatted about politics, the cost of good color paints, his father's hatters shop, the myth of the Starmen (both the academic version and the popular), his personal belief for the collapse of the Golden Age (poisoning of the 'radiawaves'), when the fad for Chargoose feathers would pass, and whether investing in new iron fields would pay off in the short term.

Jerry held his book and made interested noises, but barely made any progress in his reading.

A sturdy man in rustic clothes walked in to join them. "Why are you here?" he demanded.

Meade tapped his paint brush on the easel. "I have permission from the church to paint here."

"It's my land. You don't have my permission." He looked over at Jerry with a critical eye, and frowned.

Meade set aside his brushes. "See here. I spoke with the Speaker and the Port Master, and the Mayor. They all said that as long as I was respectful and touched nothing, I could make my paintings in peace."

The shepherd waved his hand at Meade, "Come back tomorrow. You're not wanted here now."

He spoke directly to Jerry. "Are you painting, too?"

"No. I was reading," he held up his book, "and admiring your red sheep."

Meade frowned at the sky. "The light is going, anyway. I'd better pack up."

The shepherd barely paid him any attention. Jerry was nervous under the unwavering scrutiny. "I appreciate the bench here. It was very comfortable."

Meade gathered his supplies and reached out his hand to say goodbye. Jerry stood and said, "It's been a pleasure to listen to all you've had to say."

Meade nodded and left. He loaded his stuff on a small cart that he pulled himself and began the way back to town.

"Are you leaving, too?" asked the landowner.

Jerry was in a bind. Lil would likely open the door to check on him sooner or later, and he didn't want to leave and have her confront the shepherd. But what excuse would he have to stay?

"I was hoping to stay here until the stars came out."

"You are staying near here?"

"Yes."

The shepherd nodded. "Then I will stay with you."

He sat down on the ground where he stood. Jerry sat back down on the bench. They stared at each other as the light began to fade.

"I have enjoyed watching the red sheep. There were no red sheep where I came from."

He nodded. "Our family has the largest flock in the world. My ancestors discovered the first red lamb on this hill. We have cared for them ever since, and we've been blessed."

It felt uncomfortable, with the man sitting before him. After his first, gruff challenge, his attitude had changed radically. There was something humble about the way he spoke.

At least he wasn't looking toward the iron door.

"Do you visit the town often?"

"I was born there, but I have built a house in the woods." He nodded towards the trees visible out the opening. "I have a wife and two daughters. I have a man in town who deals with the river merchants."

Something about the copper room caught Jerry's attention. Had it flickered in color again? He couldn't tell in the twilight.

He wanted to keep the man's attention. "It's a blessing to have children."

He nodded. "I've always been blessed." He almost said something, but hesitated.

Behind the man's head, the iron door slowly opened.

What can I do to stop her? Can't she see him?

Lil stepped out, dressed in the cheerleader outfit. What was she thinking?

"Cal?" Lil spoke quietly.

The shepherd breathed in sharply. He did not turn. "Yes, Lady."

"It is time to go home and smile at your daughters. Your guest has things to do."

He nodded and stood. He bowed to Jerry and without a look back, he left.

Jerry made a dash for the iron door and the both of them hurried inside.

Lil slapped the switch and gave it five seconds.

"How far?"

"A few years."

Year 487

He sat on a chair, nearly limp from the released tension.

"Lil, I don't know for sure, but I feel like that shepherd knew who I was."

"Oh, he did. I watched him."

Jerry gestured widely, "But how?"

She pulled the other chair up next to him and rested her head against his side. "Jerry, you're still a giant, pale skin, with a strange accent. And Cal noticed the mended tear on your jeans, right where the legends said you were injured.

"And, well, I don't know how to say this, but Cal's family knows you stayed close to Canton."

He put his arm around her shoulder. "Uh, not to be nosey or anything, but how did you know this shepherd's name? I know he never told me."

She hesitated, with a finger on her lower lip. "Well, I guess I'd better explain something."

...

He listened quietly, and then added his own information, the stories he'd gotten from Meade.

"Oh." She looked as worried as he did.

"Yeah."

They were silent for a while.

"I hate this legend stuff," he grumbled. "It isn't real."

"I'm so sorry!"

He held her hand, and when he realized she was crying, he held her close.

"Hey, none of that. Who could tell this would get out of hand? You were just doing the right thing for that shepherd family. You shouldn't ever apologize for doing a good thing for another human being."

She sniffed. "Unintended side effects. That's the worst thing about being legendary."

"Or pretend legendary."

She punched him, still sniffling. "No. You've got it wrong! There's no pretend. There's no false legendary. We are creatures of legend. For real. Get your head around that."

"But the stories they're telling...exaggerations and wild speculation."

Lil straightened up. "Suck it up, Lord Jereomy. You did things that started legends. You're still doing them! We're time travelers, and we decided to help some people. May I remind you, 'You shouldn't ever apologize for doing a good thing for another human being.'

"Just because other people make mistakes and believe their own fantasies isn't your fault. That's the result of their own unintended side effects. A legend is as much the fault of the storyteller as the principal. Maybe even more."

He sighed. "You're probably right. But can we split this century? I think I've had enough of worshipful shepherds."

"Right." She stood and went to the dials. "How far ahead?"

He closed his eyes and rubbed the bridge of his nose. "At least a hundred. I'd prefer more, but I don't want to risk missing the next technological era. We still need electricity to charge the batteries. I don't want to be stuck in the middle of some plague with no way to escape."

"Two hundred? Three?"

"Split the difference. Two-fifty. Okay?"

She hesitated and then set the dial to the high speed point. "Another thirty seconds?"

"Good enough."

She hit the switch and they listened to the whine of passing days. It changed intensity slightly from time to time and then dropped noticeably.

"I hope that's not another global winter."

Lil was counting. At thirty she turned off the switch.

Year 727

She waved to the door. "I'll let you do the honors."

He listened carefully, and then turned the latch.

Frowning, he tugged. "That felt funny."

The door resisted, and then with a metallic, tearing sound, it came open. Under the dim light of what appeared to be artificial lighting, it appeared that the door was covered in metallic foil. Gold foil.

...

"You've got to be kidding me!" They both stood in the elegant tiled atrium that held the gold covered copper room. The stone wall was still up, if showing even more wear. There was a fancy wrought iron gate sealing the opening.

And above all, a dome covered the whole, with a large portal at the very peak where stars showed faintly.

Lil began giggling.

"I don't think it's funny."

She didn't stop, gesturing to the surroundings. "Creatures of Legend. That's what we are. I guess the Doorway to Heaven needed a facelift."

Jerry stalked to the iron gateway. It was locked. And this time, there wasn't even a tree to look over the stone wall.

He went back to the iron door and started peeled the gold foil off. "Whacha doing?"

"This offends me. I'm a creature of legend. If the gold is an offering, I'm taking it."

She looked sideways and nodded. "Good enough. The worst that can happen is that they come and catch us."

"That could happen anyway. We defaced their holy artifact by opening the door in the first place."

"Okay." She took the left and he took the right.

The gold foil had been hammered into place over the copper room, but it never bonded with the copper in any way, so it was like stripping a thick aluminum foil off a wall. It peeled easily. They kept wadding the gold into balls and tossing them into the room. When they met at the back wall, they worked together and pulled the roof layer off in one large sheet. They rolled it up. Their haul felt like a hundred pounds.

There was a faint glow of dawn showing overhead when they finished.

"Well, I guess that's it." Jerry took one last look around. "Are you ready to move on?"

"Do you want to leave a message?" she asked. "How about, 'Thanks for the gold, Jereomy and Lillian?'"

"That'd just enhance the legend."

"But what if some innocent is charged with the theft?"

Jerry shook his head. "People will believe what they can believe. They can't believe something like us, so any message we left would be interpreted as a joke, or a hoax or something else. Best just leave it unexplained, just something that happened, like a tornado or any other natural disaster."

She grabbed his arm. "Good enough. Natural disasters, 'R Us. Let's go."

Year 967

Two hundred and forty years later...just as the time hum died, Lil shrieked as she fell to the floor. Jerry went sprawling as well, but landed on the bed. But that wasn't the end of it. The bed, chairs and table, and even the forlorn refrigerator all skidded to the side.

"Hang on, Lil!"

But everything, other than a stack of books, slid to a stop after a moving a foot or so.

"What happened?"

Jerry tentatively tested his footing. "The floor is tilted. Are you okay?"

He stepped over to where she lay on the floor.

"Just a bunged knee. I'll be fine."

He knelt down beside her and felt around the knee joint.

She winced when he got too close to the scrape. "I've had lots worse at cheerleader practice."

"Stay put. Where's the ointment?"

She directed him to her first aid kit and he applied the bandage.

"I'll be wearing the longer skirts until this heals."

Jerry realized his hand was still resting on her leg. Her eyes met his. He shifted position. "Let me help you up."

He took her arm and let her sit on one of the chairs that had slid all the way to the lowest wall.

"I'm okay, really. What happened to us?"

"Something moved the room. It's tilted ten degrees or more. We didn't notice it until the time field snapped off. I guess I'd better have a look."

He walked uphill to the door and cautiously opened it slightly.

There was a city outside. He closed and latched the door.

"Well, what did you see?"

He set the other chair beside her and sat down. "There's rubble all around us. The stone wall is gone, and so is the temple dome thing. About thirty yards away is a line of one story buildings, with people walking back and forth, more than I could count in my quick look.

"There were also two motorized vehicles, like small delivery trucks, driving on the road in front of the buildings."

She gripped his hand, "So we're back in a time like ours?"

"I don't know. The technology is similar, maybe. But you could say the same about the 1920's. Certainly I didn't see any electric advertising signs. I'm going to need to go out and take a better look when the light fades and I can sneak out the door without being seen. Suddenly, I miss that stone wall."

"One other thing," she said.

"Yes?"

"We're nearly out of food. A couple of pieces of bread and a stick of beef jerky. You're worried about getting electricity, but we need food and water as well."

"One thing at a time." He reached over and picked up one of the gold foil balls that had all rolled downhill as well. "I wonder if I could trade these things."

...

He eased up on twilight, flipping the switch a half-second at a time.

"Okay, keep the door latched, and be ready to jump a day if anyone but me comes to test the door."

She nodded. "1,2,4 taps is the signal."

"I'll take a short look around and come back quickly."

The presence of lighted windows was encouraging. There were a couple of people still out on the street, so he moved away from the iron door as quickly as he could manage over the rubble.

Looking back was a revelation. Someone had built a loosely constructed wall, using old stones, lumber, and evidently, old copper rooms. It stretched a half mile towards the river, and then turned south. It was about ten feet high, and he was grateful that the copper room was on the top level of the pile, rather than being its foundation. Without the time field to give it imperviousness, the copper roof could have collapsed in on them.

Who built the wall, and why did they need it?

The only things that came to mind were defense against invaders, and a barricade to keep captives in. It certainly wasn't built as a work of art. Somebody took bulldozers, or whatever the current equivalent, and just shoved whatever was available up as a berm.

I guess we were lucky it wasn't turned upside down in the process.

Note to self: don't go walking up on top of the wall. Probably there are guards with guns somewhere.

Down at street level, he tried walking like a normal person. From this vantage point, he could see the street went on until it dead-ended at the wall to the south and...yes, the same the other way. This area was inside the wall, whatever that meant.

A whiskered man in a coat and cloth hat, walking hunched up with his hands in his pocket glanced his way as they crossed. He mumbled something. Jerry just kept on walking.

The language had drifted even more. He could tell its roots were like English, but it just sounded jumbled. But maybe Lil could make sense of it. He'd been confused the first time, when they'd walked down to Canton, but it had just been a thick accent, and he could adapt to that. But at some point, even Lil would just have to acknowledge that it was a different language, something to be learned.

"Yo!" It was the man who had spoken. The call was intense and low, like he didn't want it to carry. He gestured to follow. When Jerry turned, he began walking, even faster.

When a local in a dangerous place tells you to follow him, either it's to lead you away from danger, or into a trap.

Considering that this city was beginning to look more and more like a prison and that there were hardly any people left on the street, there might be a curfew. He hesitated only an instant before following.

To his left, at the top of the barricade wall, a figure in black appeared, and walked across the only flat place, the roof of the copper room.

Lil!

But his guide noted his faltering pace and grabbed his arm and tugged him along.

Lil would hear the steps. She'd jump ahead. She'd know he wasn't coming straight back like he'd planned. Wouldn't she?

He looked again at his guide. This close up, the fur on his ears stood out. Another descendant of the werewolf. Was James Peters in his family tree?

Somehow, seeing someone who looked like Caleb Peters who'd traded shovels with him preparing the barge trap eased some of his suspicions. They ducked into a darkened alleyway, and for the first time he couldn't see the copper room.

Getting away from the city wall eased his guide's pace. They slowed to a walk as they navigated the passageway that was more like a labyrinth than a city street. They were walking through people's yards. Half the openings spilled yellow light. He saw a few candles, dousing his hopes that they were finally in an era that would let him charge the batteries. The last time he checked, the bank of batteries designed to run the time circuits and the air refreshing system—and which he'd abused to run a refrigerator and microwave—was just over 35% charged. Avoiding the air system made a big difference, but right now Lil was stuck inside and it was dangerous to open the door. She might have to refresh the inside air, and that would suck it dry in a matter of a few hours.

And this didn't look like a good period to be stuck in.

They ducked under several successive clothes lines, strung from one house to another across the walkway, and his guide turned into a doorway that was nearly invisible, hidden as it was on the back wall of the building.

Jerry followed him in, and pushed aside a blanket stretched across a hallway as a secondary door.

A dozen sets of eyes looked at him suspiciously. His guide had moved up to the bar and was having a whispered conversation with someone bundled up like it was deep winter. The others were seated at a trio of candle-lit tables against the other wall. The place was decorated with old paintings, a burning oil lamp, and other kinds of wall hangings. A bright copper-hued placard said, "CANTON DEUMER" over an ornate seal of some kind.

One of the hangings was a blood red flag with a white 'C' in the middle. That brought back some memories.

And behind the far table seemed to be an exercise bicycle.

His guide was still talking about him, pointing his way from time to time. Jerry edged across the room to take a look at the machine.

That's a generator. He could see coils arranged like spokes and wires going to a split commutator. There must be magnets in the fork. The whole thing was too small for someone his size, but if there was one, in a bar, then there were likely others. He had to find out how to get one.

The wadded gold foil in his pocket probably wasn't enough, but as soon as he could manage the language, that was his first priority.

He reached down and gave the wooden paddle a push. A dozen lights in the room flickered dimly as the spokes spun through the fork.

"Hey! Nontat!" A man hopped up from the table and stopped the spinning wheel. Everyone was tensed.

"Sorry. I was just trying it out."

"Billesly?" asked another of the men sitting at the table, holding a mug.

Jerry smiled and shrugged. "I'm afraid I don't speak the language."

His guide stepped over and pulled him by the arm over to the bar.

This close, the candle light showed the man under the heavy coat to be bald with thin features. His skin looked wrinkled and old, but there was no facial hair at all. It was especially noticeable next to the hair covered man next to him.

The old man reached across to touch his face. "Albin?"

Was that albino?

Jerry shook his head and fingered his own hair and tugged down a lower eyelid to show off his brown eyes. "No. Just pale."

The old man asked more questions, but it was all just a jabber to him. He shrugged a lot.

His werewolf guide gestured expansively at his size.

That again. Although these city dwellers were maybe a little larger than the riverside farmers he'd met five hundred years before, he was again the giant.

The bald leader, behind the bar, pointed to his guide and from the general tone, Jerry guessed that since he was the one who'd picked up the stray, he was being put in charge of him.

No longer being questioned, Jerry went from picture to picture on the wall, trying to make out what was being shown in the dim light. He wondered why the electric lights were off limits, but it might be part of the curfew. Could the lights inside be visible to the outside? The curtain in the entranceway made more sense if so.

After looking at numerous sketches and paintings of people who were just more unknown faces, he came across a map of the town. It was certainly larger than he remembered from his last visit. And the roads were different from when he had discovered the way to Uncle Greg's house when he was first learning to drive. A couple of the main roads were nearly the same, probably following the road base that might have survived from his era.

The church grounds were marked, with four buildings where there had been one. Down at the riverfront, there were docks and large storage buildings. The near side of the dam was marked, with an elaborate lock system showing.

Up on the far side was a square within a square. In nearly illegible hand lettering was marked "Dr. 2 Hvn." *Door to Heaven?* There was no sign of the temple dome. Was this map that old?

He looked around. His guide was sipping from a mug.

"Um. I have a question?" The man studiously ignored him.

"Band?" It was the short, heavyset man that had stopped the generator before.

Jerry pointed at the map. "How old is this?"

There was just smiling puzzlement.

Jerry took a different tack. "Where is the city wall?"

He traced the path he'd seen slowly across the map, being careful not to touch it.

The smile went away. Stern distaste replaced it. The short man nodded and finished the path of the wall that Jerry hadn't seen in person. It made a large square, a couple of miles across.

"What is it for?" He tapped the unseen wall and shrugged.

Several of the others were watching the pantomime and their comments made it clear their opinions on the matter were as one. They all hated it.

It was a prison then. But why?

"Why?" he asked out loud.

The chubby man exchanged looks with his drinking buddies.

The old man at the bar had apparently been watching. He stepped up and shrugged off his heavy coat. The man was thin, really thin, like a walking skeleton. But for all that, he didn't look emaciated. It was just his natural form.

He then pulled his guide closer by the ear and made sure Jerry saw the hairy skin.

Next was another man at the tables who pulled off his cap to show pointed ears. Another showed off his dalmatian-like natural spots, just like a guy at home would have proudly shown his tattoos.

And the old man put his coat back on and pointed to Jerry. "Albin." And he went back to the bar.

So. It is a race thing. Jerry felt his face get hard.

Others saw the anger and nodded. He was like them.

Somehow, in this area, the different ones, the werewolves, the skeleton men, the dog men, the elves, the dwarves, and the white kid were rounded up into a ghetto, under guard.

Were they waiting there to die out, or was a pogrom planned?

. . .

The werewolf's home was even deeper into the interior of the walled area than the bar. Jerry had to duck his head as he entered. It was almost a replay of his introduction at the bar, except his wife was the one with the questions, and a boy about 12 and a girl a couple of years younger were the eyes at the table.

They appeared to be having school. A blackboard was propped against the wall and 58 X 217 = remained unworked. The mother looked on cautiously as he picked up the chalk and to the kids' grins, he worked it for them.

The young faces seemed interested, so he scribbled out a fairly simple long division problem and handed the chalk to the boy. He worked it in short order. It wasn't quite the way he'd done it in elementary school, but the results were fine.

Encouraged that at least the language of mathematics hadn't changed in nearly a thousand years, he tested their limits.

1+2+3+...+99+100=

That got a big sigh from the boy and a panicky look in the little girls eyes. The both of them were lightly furry faced. The boy looked like he had a lightly trimmed beard, but it was easy enough to ignore it.

Had the werewolves consistently married within their own kind? Or was the trait dominant, and came out even when they married bare-skinned sweethearts? There had to be many novels with that as a theme.

Certainly, even as Lil had noticed long ago, the women carried it off well. There was nothing bestial about their features.

The boy went up to the board and started working the problem the hard way. Jerry put his hand on his shoulder and rubbed out the partial work with the rag. He then wrote:

1+100=101

2+99=101

...

49+52=101

50+51=101

50 X 101 = 5050

The girl squealed in delight and punched her brother. He, of course, punched back. The mother and father, who had been watching the interplay quietly, called the children down.

He picked up their names. Sally and John.

The mother invited him over to their table and asked him something. He shrugged and smiled. "I don't speak the language."

She mimed eating.

Oh. He patted his stomach, and it obediently growled.

They laughed. She went to her pots and testing the heat of her oven, simmered some crushed grain. She sighed when she measured the grain, and then added an additional portion.

One more data point. Food was rationed or scarce. He regretted the necessity of accepting their hospitality.

By pointing, and with the kids' names as examples, he soon discovered his guide was named David and his wife was Clare. He offered them Jerry. Surely there was no risk in them connecting him to the five hundred year old Lord Jereomy.

The meal was satisfying. As he ate, he watched John working at the blackboard on his own. He added 1 through 10, both ways, and when they were the same, he struggled through 1 through 20. By the time his mother sent him to bed, he had even tried 50 through 60, proving to himself that the method was trustworthy even when you didn't start with 1.

"John is smart."

They understood what he said, if not the words.

As the candles were being put out, one by one, Jerry noticed a round fixture on the wall. He pointed and asked, "What is that?"

David shook his head sadly. He pointed at an ornate fixture in the corner. Jerry looked closely and discovered that it was a dusty lamp with a cord. The bulb was a flat fixture of some kind, not a filament bulb, but something else. The plug was like a cone that could be twisted into the wall socket, with a center tip and an outside sleeve. The house was wired for electricity, but it was all turned off. From the presence of the generator at the bar, it was likely the electricity was gone from the whole town, and likely banned.

"David, you could plug this cord into the generator couldn't you?" He mimed the action with the real lamp cord and an imaginary generator making big slow circles.

He nodded, but his words likely said it was useless because there weren't any generators to be had.

...

He slept next to the blackboard on the floor, with a loaned blanket and a pillow. It was much better than sleeping on a pile of hay, but he really missed Lil.

He hoped she was okay.

In the middle of the night, with the house dark and silent, he woke and couldn't get back to sleep. Time travelers never had a good lock on day and night. That took staying in the same pattern for days on end, and he didn't even want that to happen yet.

Like before, the people were fine, but this was a horrible era for Lil. Did David and his family even know the history of pogroms? Were they waiting patiently for something to change for the better? Or did they know it was just a matter of time before those outside came in with torches and weapons to get rid of them? It was times like this that he wished he hadn't read so many history books.

And who were those outside? Was this a local prison? Just one of thousands to contain a large population of altered humanity? Or was this the last remaining compound in the whole world? Were the jailers just the ones that had gotten an upper hand, or were they professionals backed by a world government?

If people like David made a break for it, would there be places to hide? Was there a land just over the hills with more tolerance, or was that a fantasy?

There wouldn't likely be refuge close at hand, not if this many people were being starved out in such a systematic way. And he hadn't seen any hope in the attitudes of David or his bar buddies.

Sleep was impossible. He moved quietly to the front door and stared at the stars. With the likelihood of a curfew, he couldn't roam, so he just leaned against the doorpost, ready to jump back inside if there was any movement.

In spite of all the years, there were still satellites, including that big one, crossing the familiar star field. The numbers had dropped, but he supposed that was to be expected if space travel had been lost along with the other technologies.

Was there a scientist, or even a full fledged national space program somewhere, working to recover the technology that had been lost? What would they discover once they reached that space station that had been orbiting faithfully for hundreds of years?

He frowned. But...

"Jerry," came a quiet voice.

He turned. David had come to see what he was doing.

Pointing at the receding light of the station, he asked, "What is that?"

David looked, puzzled. "Munat."

"Munat?"

He nodded. He gestured to the west, where the moon was hovering above the horizon. "Mun." He pointed toward the northeast where the station had disappeared, "Munat." He made a big circle with his hands. "Mun." And then a tiny one. "Munat."

So. As far as David was concerned, it wasn't a space station, just a little moon, no more worthy of interest than the big one.

He supposed it wasn't much different with his school buddies back at his home time. When they saw a satellite move in the sky, they probably just thought it was an airplane or something.

David asked him something. He pointed to the glow on the horizon. Jerry shrugged and smiled. Without knowing what he wanted, it was all he could do in this situation.

. . .

Soon, David was dressed for the day, and they waited patiently in the doorway for the first ray of sunlight. Then he gestured and they headed out.

When the wall came into view, he was relieved to see no activity near the dirty copper-toned cube. They hadn't attracted any attention. That was good.

But what about Lil? Had she been waiting for him? He paused as they hit the street. Was the iron door open, just a hair?

"Jerry?" asked David, wondering what he was looking at.

Slowly, as if he were just stretching his muscles, he made a swing of his arm in a full circle. If she were watching, would she understand? *Go ahead another day.*

There was a faint flicker of color. He sighed. She was safe. She knew he was okay. And she was invulnerable for another day.

. . .

David was a delivery driver. They arrived at a locked parking lot with five of the vehicles. Other drivers were showing up as well. The albino giant attracted some attention, but not much commentary.

David opened the engine cover and fired up the burner. By the smell of it, the fuel was alcohol, and it heated a boiler full of water. Soon, there was enough steam pressure, and with Jerry bending down as small as he could to get into the cab, the two of them puttered out onto the street.

They approached the downhill leg of the city wall, and pulled up to the warehouse that was built just outside the entrance. Armed guards watched from towers.

In a thousand years, they still hadn't invented a portable, long range killing weapon any better than a rifle. He couldn't see the details, so it might be a marvel of engineering for all he knew, but he could see at a glance that it was a projectile weapon that wouldn't be too much out of place in his home time.

He didn't want to get any closer to the guards than he had to. Instead, he watched as David presented a paper list and a small stack of copper coins and a necklace to the quartermaster.

The necklace was inspected and they haggled over its worth. Knowing what was going on, half the words made sense. The quartermaster questioned whether the silver chain was real silver or just silver-plated. David demanded that he test it, right there.

Eventually, a price was named, and entered in a log book.

David's list was signed and they moved on to the warehouse. There, David handed it to a worker and bags of grain were wheeled out. Jerry took the hint and helped carry the bags to the truck. With two workers, they were quickly done, and drove back into the city.

When he looked at the other truck drivers, it was clear the pattern was pretty consistent. It was a one-way trade. Cash and valuables for basic supplies. There were grain and bolts of cloth and cans of something that was probably the alcohol fuel. Canton likely had its own water wells, but they were dependent on everything else.

It was all too clear what was going on. The captors would bleed away all the cash, and every item of value that the prisoners owned, until there was nothing left. David and his friends and family would begin starving themselves to stretch out what valuables they possessed. When they were too weak to do anything, an 'accident' would happen, and the town would burn to the ground and the guards could claim innocence.

The clock was ticking. He could see it all too clearly, but he couldn't think of a thing to do. Disarmed, the altered ones could do nothing to break themselves free. They would try, he was sure, but only when they were too hungry and weak to make it work.

The deliveries were predictable. David drove routes through the town, sticking to the wider streets that could handle the truck. He called out, "Wheat! Wheat for sale!" over and over. Of course, the words were pronounced a little different, but Jerry was sure he had the translation correct.

David sold to housewives by the scoop. Everyone haggled over the price, and some were angry, as if the price had gone up.

David was a middleman, able to turn a profit and get supplies for his family at a discount, but if he weren't careful, people would start identifying him with their oppressors. He'd need to play a careful game. And even then, the end was the same.

About noon, they paused to get food at an open-air stall near the warehouse. Jerry fingered the ball of gold foil in his pocket, but he would have to be careful who saw it. He let David pay for his lunch, a roll of flatbread like a flour tortilla seasoned with something he couldn't place. It was slightly fishy, but that could have been from the oil with which it was made.

The afternoon run had a couple of notable deliveries. They ran two full bags of wheat up to the church on the bluff. David was respectful and haggled less with the hairless Speaker, a man of the same skeletal genetic pattern as the owner of the bar.

Jerry went to the overlook. From this vantage point he could see over the walls. To the north was an active city of its own, and across the waters, he could see the trail of smoke from smokestacks. Did the outsiders have their own church? And did they do anything to help their brothers inside?

Jerry shook his head. It would be far too easy to become bitter in this place.

David called, and he hurried back to the truck.

The last delivery of the day was to a man with a hand-cart.

"Albin," nodded the old man in heavy coats. It was the bartender. He took a full bag of grain and paid quickly with no haggling. The bar must have been close, but the regular entrance was on a passageway much too small for the truck.

After that, they drove back to the parking depot. David tallied up accounts with the company overseer and watched as his vehicle was fueled up and the water tank topped off. They walked out with a small bag of grain for his wife, Clare.

David was pleased. He pointed to the setting sun, it was still light since they'd finished earlier than normal.

Jerry pointed, "Munat." David squinted and nodded. The moonlet/station was bright enough to be seen in daylight if you were looking for it.

Jerry didn't pause as they passed by the copper room. The door was shut tight, and somewhere inside Lil was motionless, with no detectable heartbeat or breathing, suspended in a different time rate, impervious to harm.

He looked for the bar, but passed it without noticing the entrance until David gestured toward it.

He nodded, and they walked in. Jerry waved aside any drink. He was more interested in the generator.

Some of the regulars nodded to him and he greeted them with, "Hey." Careful not to touch anything, he smiled when he saw the wiring. It was normally plugged into the wall socket and fed power back into the house wiring, but there was a switch.

He grinned and spoke to the bar owner, "Can I trace this wire?"

"Albin, Albin." He sighed, and then gave permission with a gesture.

He followed the wire tacked to the baseboard and entered a darkened closet. Enough candle light leaked in to confirm his suspicion. It was a vacuum still.

There was a wooden barrel which probably contained fermenting grain mash. After it reached appropriate ripeness, the mash would be fed into the chamber and sealed. An electric pump reduced the air pressure until the mix boiled, and from there, the vapors cooled in copper tubes, separating the ethanol from the water and other chemicals.

The machine was the core of this place's business—with no imports other than staples and poisonous fuel alcohol coming into the city. Even if electricity were illegal, he imagined someone was regularly pedaling away in the dead of night. If the place were raided and the generator discovered, the owner could claim it was never used, since all the lighting was done with candles and lanterns.

The owner was watching him. When Jerry looked up from his inspection of the equipment, he tapped his bald noggin.

"Smart," Jerry agreed.

...

After Sally and John were put to bed, Jerry gestured, "David?"

He came to see what his visitor was doing with the blackboard. Clare dried her hands and joined them as well.

First, he drew a big wide arc across the bottom of the board and added some stick figures.

"David. Clare. John. Sally."

Clare giggled at the little skirts on the girls.

Then in the upper left hand of the board he drew a stylized crescent moon. Then, in the middle of the board, he drew a fat dot. "Munat."

They nodded, puzzled at what he was getting at.

Lastly, he added a couple of stick figures on Munat, and then looked at his hosts.

David looked at Clare and shrugged. She tried not to smile. "Stamen."

"Right. Starmen. Do you think there are people on Munat?"

Clare got up and reaching up on her tip toes, she patted him on the head like a little kid.

Firmly, she pointed at the blanket and pillow and told him to go to sleep.

...

So, Starmen were fairy tales for kids. The beliefs had been trending that way when Meade talked his ear off back when. The scholars believed that men had been in space, once. The general populace had turned those tales into mythology. It had gotten even more unbelievable by this era. Everyone saw the moving lights in the sky, but they had always been there. If Grandpa thought they were just little moons, then that was good enough for them.

Jerry wiped the board and said softly, "David?"

He looked up, nearly dozing.

With minimal sketching, he quickly drew a map of the town, with the wall as it's boundary. He added the river and the warehouses for positioning. Then he drew a cross section of the wall and a tunnel underneath the wall.

David watched with a serious frown. He stood and took the chalk. He drew boxes where the armed guard stations were near the warehouse, then drew more boxes, nearly twenty, marking known guard stations around the perimeter of the wall.

With short, fast strokes, he drew a line from the tunnel diagram to a specific position to the south of town. Then he drew many stick figures, fifteen or twenty, and drew a big X through them.

David didn't look him in the eyes as he wiped the whole board clean. The story was plain. He hadn't been the first to think about an escape tunnel. It had been tried, and even with decent knowledge of where the guard towers were, many men had died in the attempt.

With the board cleared, David shrugged, and then went on to bed.

...

Jerry dreamed of smuggling one family at a time out of the city in the copper room and coming back for more. He woke again in the middle of the night with the fantasy banished. Only in dreams could he go backward in time. At best, he could take a half dozen or so forward into the future, leaving the rest to die. And in that future, would they be any more welcome?

David found him at the doorway again as morning drew near.

He asked if he were ready to work again today.

Jerry reached into his pocket and pulled out the ball of gold and handed it to him.

"For you and Clare and John and Sally."

David peered at the gold, nearly a couple of ounces worth, in the dim lighting. After a moment's doubt, he knew what it was. It was food and supplies and extra life for his family. Jerry could see him thinking, planning, calculating how to get the most benefit out of the windfall.

He hid it away in his pocket and gave Jerry a big hug.

But it was essential that they keep to the work schedule. They started off the same way, and when they reached the wall, Jerry's eyes were straining in the early morning light to see the iron door.

"David, wait."

He frowned, but Jerry dashed towards the copper room the instant he saw the door open a crack. Lil was waiting. He dashed inside and latched the door behind him.

"That man saw you."

"I know." Jerry dialed the settings and froze the outside world.

Lil hugged him, "I was so worried about you."

He hugged back. "How long has it been for you?"

"Several hours. I made a dozen little jumps, and I just saw your signal to jump 24 hours. What went wrong?"

He shook his head. "It's a nasty business. Let's sit down."

They pulled up chairs, side by side, which was the only way to do it on the tilted floor.

He described the situation—the city walls and the guard towers. He explained why Canton was a prison and what he believed was being played out. He pulled a couple of books from his library stash and let Lil read the descriptions of what had happened in Russia, Poland, Armenia and dozens of other places.

"I can't be too surprised that this is happening. It has happened before and probably will happen again. It's just part of the dark side of human nature."

Lil was flushed with the newness of her anger. "But just for being different. It's not fair."

"It's because they are different. Just another of those unintended consequences. People who invented mutagenics so many hundreds of years ago probably never saw this coming."

He sighed. "I can't say the newness of it all hasn't affected me. Yes, people like David, and the Peters back in the farming village of Canton are different but they're an attractive variant. Others, like the thin hairless people take more getting used to. There's an eeriness to it, with people just outside the comfortable boundaries of what we're used to. Let me work beside them for a week or a month, and we'll be buddies, but it takes effort.

"In the best of worlds, we'd grow up with our definitions of 'people' wide enough to cover them all. Sadly, for many, a bad experience or two would be enough to make 'them versus us' a natural course."

Lil was still looking over the book. "Ethnic differences. It makes me ashamed I never reached out to Carla Gonzales at school." She sighed and closed it. "So, what are we going to do?"

He took her hand. "That's why I came to talk to you."

. . .

"We could, right now, jump far enough into the future that this whole ugly mess would just be a footnote in another history book."

She looked at the book in her hands. "It's different when you're there. I don't want to leave people to die without at least trying to help."

He nodded. "Same here. Another choice is to unload this gold foil littering the place and give it to David and his friends. If they were extremely lucky, they could use it extend their life and maybe bribe enough people to get some to safety."

"The Schindler's List solution," she nodded. "But what if they're not lucky?"

"Then the sudden presence of gold showing up in the market would make some overseers greedy and they just might increase raids and inspections and move up the final purge."

Lil looked like she'd eaten something rancid. "That would be tricky. What else could we do?"

"Invite a handful of people to escape to the future."

She looked pale. "Jerry, I understand, but I'm not sure we should do that."

"Your reasons?"

"Once you flip the switch and hear the whine, everybody outside dies. We've gotten used to it. I'm comfortable with it. But I'm still not over the loss of my parents and my school friends. That first step is a trauma. I wouldn't wish it on anyone.

"If you friend David and his family jumped with us, they'd know their friends died, and not only that, they'd know that they left them to die horribly.

"I can't do that to anybody. You can overrule me, but it's a horrible decision to make. Anything else?"

Jerry sighed. "There's a pedal-powered electric generator in the bar where David's friends hang out. It would be enough to solve our electricity problems and I'd toyed with the idea of buying it with enough gold to tempt the bar owner give it up.

"Unfortunately, I don't think I can stomach it. It's too much like being a vulture, picking over the dying flesh, making off with the valuables while the city dies."

Lil nodded. "I understand. We'll get our electricity some other way."

"And after that, I've only got one last idea, and it's so off the wall and out of the box that it's closer to praying for a miracle than an actual plan."

She looked up at him. "Sounds interesting. What is it?"

...

David saw Jerry go inside the Doorway to Heaven, and then come right back out a second later with a bag over his shoulder. The door closed behind him, and it was so outlandish that he was ready to blink his eyes real hard and call it a momentary hallucination. Everyone knew the Door wasn't real, just a sculpture carved on the side.

Jerry put his hand on David's shoulder. "Go on to work by yourself. I can't go with you today." He turned back and headed the way they came.

...

The old man looked out from his coat and asked what he was doing there this time of day.

"Sir, my name is Jerry. I've got a business proposition to make you."

The bar was empty this time of day, and it looked like he'd woken the man up.

"Bizniz?"

Jerry pulled out a sheet of gold the size of a sheet of paper.

The wrinkly hands picked it up in a flash, and held it to the light. He was suddenly all attention. He locked the door behind them and led the way to the tables.

Jerry took a deep breath. He had a lot to cover and he had to do it mostly with pictures. He pulled out the first spiral notebook, with all the homework assignments stripped out and new drawings added.

"This is Munat. There are Starmen who live there."

...

By the time that David was done with his day's work and arrived at the bar, there were five people there, passing around the three notebooks and discussing the proposal.

Jerry had a headache. He'd argued all day long, sometimes over the words and their meanings, sometimes over whether the idea was preposterous.

He'd forced himself to believe it, or he'd never have gotten them to consider it in the first place.

"Yes, you can make the signal light where the guards can't see it. See here." He flipped to the diagram where a long barrel had an array of the 'lightbulbs' at the deep end. The light would only come out in one direction, and the barrel could be steered to track Munat in the sky.

One man would have to keep the light beam aimed at Munat. One man would have to pedal the generator, and still a third would have to key the code.

There was another question about that. Jerry showed the Morse Code chart that he'd copied out of one of his books. Luckily the alphabet was the same, and even many words in the printed versions. It turned out it was English, just a little more warped by the thousand years that had passed. It was just that their accents and some grammar had drifted so much that neither could understand the other without a lot of practice.

He had written out a suggested message for them: "SOS. SOS. SOS. Canton is being starved to death for our differences. We appeal to the men from the stars, our brothers, to rescue us."

A few more hours and he would have them convinced that if they could secretly blink that light to the space station overhead night after night, that the Starmen would understand it and come to their aid. He almost believed it himself.

Ason, the bar owner, would take the greatest risk, and keep it running for as long as it took. And for that, he would receive twenty pounds of gold foil.

It ought to work. That station is in an extraordinarily stable orbit. I've seen it move the same way, with the same orbital period since that first night in the Regat's park. Nothing with an orbital period that fast could stay stable for hundreds of years without adjustments to overcome atmospheric drag. And even last night, I could see other dots pacing it through the sky. Even if the space colonists have broken off connection with the Earth, surely they would be curious about a blinking light below.

Blink the light and pray. It was the only thing that he could suggest. Anything else was just waiting for the slaughter.

...

David entered the room. Jerry woke with a start, realizing he'd dozed off.

"It's time?"

Ason hurriedly swept the papers up and hid them behind the bar. They'd talked so much through the night that Jerry understood when he said that he was coming with them. That was no surprise. Jerry had left final payment with Lil, just in case things hadn't worked out.

The hand cart slowed things up. Ason was weaker than most men, which is why he needed the cart wherever he went. Jerry was ready to pull the cart himself, but something in the way David acted—pointedly not looking whenever Ason hit a bump and had to struggle to regain his momentum—told him there was a history there. He had to trust in Lil, even if he wasn't there at the exact time they'd agreed on.

The narrow passageway opened up onto the street, and David paused. There were a couple of guards struggling with a tripod-mounted rifle on the top of the copper room.

David signaled for them to wait. Jerry got the impression that there were armed guards on the top of the city wall every night, but this appeared unusual.

Others were coming out onto the street, and then hurrying on about their business as soon as they saw the guards.

"David, do you need to go on to start your deliveries?"

There was a frown on the man's face, but he shook his head. They would wait.

Time ticked by slowly. From what Jerry could see, the guards were trying to disassemble or pick up the rifle, but with no luck.

I wonder. There was that puzzle about how the second layer of copper skin had bonded to the original one. Could the tripod have somehow been caught up in the time field?

Uncle Greg had explained that the copper room allowed the area inside the electric conductor to be affected by the time shift. If a metal object was in contact with the copper walls when the field was turned on, then it was *possible* that the new metal object would become part of the time-shifted object.

He nodded. It made sense. Lil had dropped out of the time skip before the guards had left. She heard footsteps on the roof and jumped again, snagging the tripod.

Now the guards can't collect their weapon, and they dare not leave it behind, or their prisoners would grab it.

It all depended on how far ahead Lil skipped.

He touched David and Ason. "In just a moment, the tripod will come free, and then they will leave."

David nodded, but the bar owner was less optimistic. But regardless, all they could do was wait.

The three of them weren't the only ones using that passageway, and seeing them hide behind the corner, others were giving them suspicious looks.

Jerry smiled at a housewife who passed by them, but the instant she saw the guards, she collected her skirts and hurried on her way.

Motion behind a rain barrel caught his eye. Some kid was hiding back there, he was sure. He closed his eyes and rubbed the bridge of his nose. Nothing was going smoothly this morning. It was risky enough letting David and Ason see the door open, but random strangers? There was always the chance that people would give information to their captors in exchange for extra food or other benefits. The world was never totally black and white, your team and my team. Everybody saw the world through a different set of filters. Everybody's playbook was a little different.

And then he saw it. The color flicker.

"Now," he whispered. And sure enough, the guard straining to free the tripod yanked it up so abruptly that he fell backwards.

Hold on, Lil. Be patient.

One guard was quick to carry the rifle away, down the back side of the wall. The other remained for just a moment, examining the copper beneath him for any sign of the snag that had caused them to miss their schedule.

There was a shout, far too distant to make out, and the last guard was gone.

"Okay," Jerry took a step, but David held him for another few seconds, and then released him.

Jerry walked boldly to the edge of the rubble, waiting until he could see a crack in the door. And there it was. He climbed, carrying his bag.

"I'm ready for the payment," he whispered. She stuffed it through the gap. It was a hefty lump and hopefully no one saw the glint of gold.

He carried it down, and emptied it into Ason's hand cart, where it was instantly covered in burlap.

"I'm going now," he told them, and then to David, he whispered, "keep Ason honest."

With a glance down the street, wincing at a couple of walkers who might or might not be watching, he dashed back up to the iron door, slipped in, latched it and quickly froze the outside world.

...

Her eyes showed it all. "Oh, Jerry, I heard noises..."

"Armed guards on the roof. They put a machine gun up over night."

She nodded, "I panicked. I hit the switch for an instant..."

"Locking the rifle's tripod to the roof, tangled in the time field somehow. It didn't let go until you released it."

"Oh. But they're gone now?"

"Yes. And we're safe right now, so I've got a moment to catch my breath. By the way, you did everything exactly right. If you could hear the guards on the roof, they could likely hear you moving around inside."

"I held my breath, when I finally got the nerve to test the door. I was afraid my heart beating was making too much noise."

"It was nerve wracking from my viewpoint as well."

"How did it go?" she asked.

Jerry shook his head, "I really don't know." He settled into the tilted chair. "I gave them the plans. I'm pretty sure they understood them, and the barkeeper has been paid off. But whether they'll follow through, or whether the lights are bright enough, or whether there really are Starmen on the space station—that's all just speculation."

"You did your best." She sat beside him and held his hand.

"Maybe."

"It's never good enough for you, is it?" She griped. "I'll have you know you're a stick-in-the-mud when you're in the process of saving the world. Where's the happy, snarky, fun-loving guy I snuck out of the house to make out with?"

He looked at her with a skeptical eye. "Is that why you came over? I though it was to get some homework done?"

She moved over to sit in his lap. Arms around his neck, she kissed him.

"Watch the knee. It still stings," she mumbled after a moment.

It was her stomach growls that caused her to come up for air. "Um. Jerry. Did you manage to get any food?"

He sighed, and gave her a pat on the rump. "No. Sorry. I was caught up in the negotiations, and Ason's bar wasn't a place to get food anyway. I guess we need to decide how far ahead to jump."

She slid out of his lap, and moved to the controls.

"Short or long?"

"I don't know. The technology right now is different, but nearly equivalent to what we had at home. I'd hate to jump too far and run into another dark age. But I'm afraid to make a short jump and open the door to a graveyard."

He pulled himself out of the chair and walked over to the equipment racks, which thankfully had been bolted to the floor.

"Battery level is down to 19%." He looked pained. "I don't think we can risk a big jump until we get some way to recharge the batteries."

Lil nodded. Betting on a long shot when lives were at stake was tough. Even tougher was to actually face the results. "Okay, one year, five?"

He shrugged. "Can you make it twenty-five? It has to be over by then."

She felt his pain. Best to get it over with. She switched off the frozen time, set the dial to high speed and turned it on.

"Wait! We need to brace..."

But the three seconds were up. Lil had her hand on the wall when the floor shifted back to flat and level. Jerry grabbed the back of a chair.

Year 992

He let it go carefully and looked around. "Sorry, I should have thought of that before."

"Oh, I am so glad we're back to normal! You didn't have to live in a funhouse like I did."

She nodded towards the door. "Do you want to look or should I?"

He sighed. "Go ahead."

Lil moved the latch and peeked out the door.

"Jerry, you should see this."

He could hear the rumble. He moved up behind her and looked over her head.

The copper room appeared to be right in the middle of rush hour traffic. Hundreds of 'cars' were driving by. They appeared to be on a grassy island in the middle of the highway.

"Either the room moved, or the Mississippi River did."

She nodded. They appeared to be within a hundred yards of the water. Iron barges could be seen coming up river.

He pushed it closed. "Well, we'll have to wait until dark, if we don't want all those people seeing us walk out the door."

With his arm on her shoulder, he asked, "Are we totally out of food?"

She nodded. "I saved you half a jerky stick, but that's it. And we'll need water too."

"Go ahead and finish off the jerky and if it's okay, I'd like to take a little nap? I really didn't get any sleep last night. I haven't had a mattress in, what, three days?"

"Only if I can join you."

"Fine, but don't get me wound up. I really need the rest."

...

They jumped to midnight, in hopes that the traffic would have died down.

"That's interesting," he said, as he opened the door.

"What?"

"Come look."

Side lit, by a lamp on the side of the road, someone had put up a large advertising poster, right in front of the iron door.

What was really interesting was that the side facing them, the one hidden from the road, read, "Just in town from downriver, or from another time? Curious why the Doorway to Heaven has been moved to the shoreline? Or just curious about local history? Come to the DOORWAY to HEAVEN History Museum. Any time day or night. Look towards the river."

"Are you going there?" Lil asked.

"It's written in our English. I think it's for us."

"Then let me put on my school dress, and I'm coming too. I've been cooped up inside here too long."

"Okay, but I'm going to cross the street. I'll wait for you."

With the sign giving him perfect cover, he stepped out onto the grass and waited for a car to pass. The highway was nearly empty, but he could pick his moment and not attract attention.

The history museum was lit, but looked vacant. Still, it was worth a shot.

Lil appeared and closed the door behind her. He held his hand up, and then when a funny truck that looked hinged on its middle set of wheels passed by, he flagged her on.

They were in a city. Buildings ten stories tall, at least, were dotted all over the place.

"We're still in Canton," Lil said, pointing to the bluff in the distance, where a white church was lit up.

They walked to the museum. The entrance had signs in two languages. One of them was very familiar. "If you read Golden Age English, press the button four times."

Lil did so.

A light came on down the hallway, and a man appeared, hurrying toward the door.

Jerry was shocked to see the fur on his face.

"David?" he asked, when the door was unlocked.

He smiled. "No, John, his son. Come on in. I've been waiting for you."

. . .

"So you were the kid hiding behind the barrel!"

He nodded, handing Lil a second helping of apple pie. "I knew Dad was up to something, especially the night when you didn't come back. Sally and I had been looking for you, but when we asked, Dad was very tight lipped. He and Mom had a very intense conversation that we couldn't hear. So when he left for work, I followed."

He shook his head. "That was the most memorable day of my childhood." He grinned, "Not only because I couldn't sit down for a week after Dad saw me."

"So, are your parents...?"

He shook his head. "No. Just Sally and me. I did have a wife, but she thought I was a little crazy in the head after I spent everything to set up this place across the street from the Doorway to Heaven.

"By the way, do I have permission to call Sally to come over and see you?"

"I would love to see her."

He hopped up and dashed to the other room. They could hear bits of the conversation. "I told you they would come....no, it's not like the last time. And she's here. I told you she would be with him."

. . .

"So, John, tell me about Golden Age English." Jerry sipped the Groast, which tasted like carbonated cinnamon coffee. He didn't like it, but John thought he would.

"Oh, it's a nerdy popular language at the university level. There are still lots of books from your time period. Of course, only a few of us actually speak it. Once I decided to write my book, I knew I had to master it."

"You're writing a book?"

"Wrote it. Want to see. It's radical!" He jumped up and dashed out of the room.

Lil whispered. "Does he ever stop moving?"

"Be polite. This is a big deal for him."

John came back and unwrapped a hard bound volume. He presented it.

Jerry looked at the embossed cover.

"Lord Jereomy and Lady Lillian and the Doorway to Heaven"

Lil looked, "Oh, it's about us!"

John nodded, beaming. "Yes, I'm the world authority on you two."

Lil plucked the book from his hand and opened it up. "Oh. I can't read this."

"Sorry. It's written in Common. Hang tight." John hopped up and ran to the next room and came back with a worn thin volume. "Golden Age to Common dictionary. You'll have to use it backwards, but it'll help. Bummer that they don't make a Common to Golden Age."

Jerry said, "It looks like a nicely bound volume."

John sighed, "And it cost me a bundle, too. But I wanted something that'd last on the shelves forever."

Well, I guess I won't ask how many were sold, then.

...

Lil and Sally immediately paired up when she arrived. Sally's Golden Age English was slower than her brother's, and she apologized.

"The scholarship was never my thing. But John had to have someone to practice with. He wanted to be ready when you showed up."

"How did he know?" Lil asked. "We chose the date almost randomly."

She answered quietly, so her brother, who was talking intently on the other side of the room, wouldn't overhear. "John has theories. He has told me that when he saw Lord Jereomy go into the Doorway to Heaven, the box changed color a little bit. He's got a camera up on the roof, waiting for it to change again. The circuit goes off every so often, and he races across the street to put up his special sign in front of the door.

"Up until now, it's always been a false alarm and after a day or so, the police either make him take down the sign, or just remove it themselves." She smiled fondly at her brother. "He pays his fine and claims that next time will be the real one."

...

"No, we signaled for two years. Dad finally let me in on the conspiracy, as some of the other men grew tired of it and gave up. I got to aim the lamp, and later, I learned the code."

"That long. I expected Ason to give up on it before the others— once he had the gold in hand."

"Dad wouldn't let him. The food began to get more expensive and some people in our sector, ignorant ones, began to be afraid of Dad, fearful he would cut them off. Dad told Ason that he'd not get any more supplies for his bar if he stopped signaling."

"Two years is a long time to work at something, something dangerous, with no sign of progress."

John had a smile that seemed to glow at times. "We had faith. Faith that the legend of Lord Jereomy coming to aid of Canton in the time of its deepest need had come to pass.

"And things were getting worse by the day. It was act in faith, or give up and die."

"What happened?"

"At first, there was nothing. Then the spotter, which was me sometimes, could see a signal from Munat. It was a bright blue. It blinked, but it was a while before they actually sent a code signal."

"What did they say?"

John spoke with reverence, "'We see you.' And believe me, the word got out! It was like a fire had swept thought Canton. Practically the whole town broke curfew, braving gunshots from the guards, to see the blinking lights from above. It got so bad, that food and supplies were cut off and guards were walking the wall at all times of the day and night.

"We told the Starmen that we were starving, and that we would all be dead soon unless they helped us. We told them how many died each day, and their names. We tried anything we could to urge them to act.

"At the same time, the outsiders began sending armed patrols through the streets, looking for the agitators who were causing trouble."

John paused. Across the room, the girls' chatter stopped as well.

"And what happened then?"

John sighed. "Dad and Ason were captured and shot. But they had hidden the generator and the lamp. We flashed the story to the sky the very next night."

Sally stood up and came to sit beside her brother. "And then," she said, "the Starmen landed a pallet of food and supplies right in the heart of the city, under a billowing parachute. The Black Guards rushed into the town, but by the time they could make their way through the blockaded streets, everything was gone."

John added, "And there were radio devices included as well. Several went into hiding among our people. Two were marked to be given to our captors."

He shrugged. "After that, it was politics. More food arrived every day, and the outsiders were told that their actions were being watched. Weapons would arrive unless they backed off, and arranged our release. Marvels from the sky were promised, but only to a government containing our people as well."

Sally said, "It wasn't an easy transition. No one trusted the other side. Still don't, really. Outside of Greater Canton, there isn't any large population of Variants. But because of our presence, the Starmen put their landing field and their embassy here. Everyone knows the whole economy of the area depends on goodwill and fair treatment, so it happens."

Lil asked, "So you're safe here."

John shrugged, "As safe as anyone, I guess. I have my shop here, and Sally has her store, and we don't get hassled by the fuzz."

Sally hugged John's head. "Except you, brother, of course, for your silly signs."

"What kind of a store?" asked Jerry. "We need supplies."

. . .

John led Jerry back into the museum room. "You can have this. It still works, but it may not be what you need."

It was a smaller version of Ason's generator. "You put a foot through a stirrup and crank the handles with both hands."

"I'm grateful." He tried out the generator, with its sample light glowing easily. It would take some experimentation and testing to see if he could actually charge the battery with it, but there weren't even any light poles on the grassy island in the middle of the highway to swipe power from. It would have to be a generator or nothing.

The girls came in, giggling. Lil pointed to a low stool. "Jerry, stand on this."

"Why?"

"Just do it."

He winced as Sally produced a fabric tape and began stretching it out, taking his measurements.

"What's going on?"

"Sally's store has a few customers that are nearly as tall as you and I begged for a contemporary set of clothes." She gestured at her school dress. "Mine are almost normal."

Sally noted down some numbers on a small pad of paper. "But I've got a few things you might like as well. Dawn is showing and I have to go by the store at opening anyway. Would you like to come with me and see what we have in stock?"

Lil looked at Jerry to read his response.

Since that first moment when he'd realized that school and home and family were lost forever, and that he was Lil's protector, he'd been constantly concerned about how she was doing, where she was, and what he should be doing to keep her safe.

He asked, "Do you have portable phones?"

John asked, "You mean like hand held radios? Some are available, but we don't have them. Sally's place is just five streets upriver and then two blocks in. It's easy walking distance."

Jerry's face made a half-hearted smile, which Lil read in an instant. "Great." She turned to Sally. "Are you ready to go now?"

. . .

"Canton has become quite a city in its own right."

John walked beside him, carrying a modern version of Ason's old hand cart. "Oh, how is it different?"

"In the Golden Age, when I was born, Canton was a comfortable small town, perhaps even smaller than it had been in an earlier age when the world's commerce moved on iron rails and on riverboats.

"This Canton," he gestured, "looks more like the St. Louis of my day." It was a little bit of an exaggeration, but the feel was the same, with the taller buildings, centered on the waterfront. In the distance, there was an elaborate building that looked like more like a government house than a business center.

John pointed up a cross street and they turned. "The best schools are still at Sloo, so I lived there for a few years when I was researching for my book. Greater Canton still has a ways to grow before we can match it, in spite of all the history that has happened here." He smiled. "All the history that you brought here. It still has a more modern look to it than Sloo."

He shook his head. "There are too many 'Artifacts' down there. You can't get a building permit for much of anything without a couple of years worth of court hearings to determine if your new factory or shop would detract from the historical impact of the neighborhood."

Jerry chuckled. "In a thousand years, not much has changed then."

. . .

He spent John's money to get bread and bottles of water and canned meat and vegetables, not neglecting to include a can opener.

"Are you planning on leaving us soon?"

That question had been on his mind constantly since he'd looked out and seen the traffic. This Canton was so close to his own era that it might be foolhardy to go on. He hadn't asked too many questions about life in this now, but with local helpers, wouldn't it be reasonable to turn their remaining stash of gold into cash and find a job and a home here? One thing he'd discovered is that knowing just a few basic facts that others didn't could make a big impact. There had to be facts that were common knowledge in his time, or facts in his stash of books, that these people had not yet rediscovered. If Sloo placed such value on historical places and things, then he could set up a business turning his expertise into a living for the both of them.

But what about Lil? What did she think? Was she ready to settle down here in this time?

From the looks of things, they'd nearly escaped their legendary status. This was a modern city that didn't have time for legends.

"John? Why did the Doorway to Heaven get moved down from the hills?"

"Politics. Part of the Articles of Restoration was that the old wall was to be totally demolished and the debris used to rebuild the new waterfront. All the old warehouses and guard towers were torn down. New docks were built and the rail yards are still expanding. The idea was give the town a fresh start.

"If you want my opinion, the outsiders wanted Canton rebuilt so we Variants would decide to stay, rather than move out into other parts of the Sector. And for the most part, it worked. The population around here is probably 70% Variant.

"But when it came to the Doorway to Heaven, people realized this wasn't just another chunk of debris that could be used to build a parking lot. Even those who laughed at the legends knew it was an Artifact. Canton's own Artifact. One that ought to be proudly displayed rather than left up on the hill.

"So, it was decided to make it a prominent feature of the new waterfront, along with the courthouse and the stadium."

"Stadium? What sports do you have?"

...

"Sorry, but I have to check on my...the Doorway. I know it's probably safe where it is, but I'm just not comfortable leaving it unattended like that."

John pushed the nearly full handcart out of the way of the door. "I understand." He licked his lips. "But...is it...is it permitted for someone...someone like me...to look inside?"

Jerry felt a war inside his gut. Paranoid to the extreme, part of him didn't want anyone new to get a hint of how the time system worked. It was their safety, and their power.

But if anyone could be trusted, shouldn't it be John? He'd built his life on top of the Legend. He was funding their supplies and giving him a generator. He'd even learned Golden Age English to be able to talk to him.

Jerry nodded, "Of course. Let's go quickly, the traffic has let up a bit."

They danced across the lanes, catching an angry glare from a truck driver.

"You're going to get a fine for this?" He pointed at the sign.

John nodded proudly. "And worth it every time. I even get more visits to the museum for a week or so after I put it up. Parents bring their kids. If enough show up, I hold lectures."

"Do you sell your books?"

John shifted his head. "Once or twice. It's expensive."

"Maybe you should do a cheap version, for the masses."

John nodded as they slipped behind the sign. "Or maybe a second edition."

Jerry gripped the handle. "Now, expect to be disappointed. It will be much less than you've dreamed."

He nodded eagerly.

Jerry slipped inside and turned on a single bulb. John came in, blinking at the dim lighting. Jerry closed and latched the door behind them and brought up more lights.

"Sorry, like I said, it's not much." Jerry felt it looked like a teenager's bedroom that a hurricane had gone through. They hadn't put the furniture back since the tilt.

"What is that?" John pointed at the equipment rack.

"Those are the devices that make this room livable when we are in a different time stream."

"And that?"

"Batteries. They store the electricity that runs these devices. They are getting low. That's why I need the generator."

"And that?"

"Gold. It's a bit messy. We haven't had time to clean it up."

"And that?"

Jerry looked embarrassed. "That's a toilet."

"Oh." John looked away, puzzled by the furniture packed tightly together.

"Would you like to help me?" Jerry asked.

While Jerry told the story of the tilt, the two of them moved the bed and the chairs and table back to their previous positions.

"I wish I had time to look at all of this."

"Time. You need time? Let me give you some."

He led John to the door and had him note the large tower clock on the side of one of the riverside docks. Then he closed the door.

"Now these are the time controls."

. . .

They sat at the table, while John tried to get his mind around all that he'd learned. "I never knew this." He seemed to be panting. The air was getting stale and it was time to open the door again.

"I thought," he breathed several times, "that you and Lady Lillian were supernatural creatures." He smiled at his own ignorance. "I mean it's not unusual to think that in the Golden Age, many superhuman beings existed. There are books, proving that they existed—Superman, Gandhi, Wolverine."

"We've never claimed to be special. We've never even claimed the titles. We're just ordinary people."

John nodded. "Yes, I know. Ordinary people with this super science. But you always left a big impression, whenever you appeared. Maybe you never claimed any special status, people just knew."

Jerry hesitated to push it. John's whole life had been built on these ideas.

"Well, it's time to get back into the normal time stream."

He stood and flipped the switch. John looked again at the distant clock and shook his head, marveling. "I could have used a place like this when I was at the University. It would make a great study room."

...

A chime was sounding when they arrived back to the museum. John left him at the door and raced to get the call.

"What is it? Okay."

He went to a box on the wall and turned a switch. A booming voice came up to full volume.

John listened and then began explaining:

"The Protective Alliance...that's the foreign groups that have been upset that we have access to the Starman trade and that they don't... they claim that they will destroy the landing zone and the Embassy.

"The announcer says the Sector Governor has ordered the population to stay calm and let the military deal with the intruders. He says that the claims of the PA to be able to destroy all of Canton with just a single ship are preposterous and just a ploy to create panic."

Jerry took his arm. "John. Where is Lil?"

"She's still with Sally. They're coming here."

"John, listen for any more details about the intruders. I'll be right back."

He dashed outside and ran towards the river.

Echoes of gunshots were rolling across the water. The hybrid child of a river barge and a twin smokestack tugboat bristled with gun barrels. Those had to be artillery. On the shore, vehicles flashing lights were collecting a defense force that seemed ready to repel any landing. The dockside flags were flying bravely.

Just one gunship. And with guns only big enough to take out other ships. There was no way they could destroy the town with just those guns.

No time. No time.

He ran back. "Update me."

John nodded. "The PA seems to have launched a battle barge somewhere on the Ohio River disguised with a false superstructure.

It was finally challenged by the Patrol, but by that time it was already in Sector waters and was able to outgun any vehicle the Patrol sent to challenge it.

"The reporter says that their ultimatum is against the Starmen. Leave or be blown up. There's a deadline, but it's not being released."

Jerry nodded. "John, what's the biggest explosion you've heard of?"

He shrugged. "I don't know. There are naval battles reported on the East coast of the continent that talk about destroying whole ships. We don't see things like that here in the interior. Do you think it's a bluff?"

"I have read about many battles."

John said, "I know! The Tale of the Lost Book. You talked to a painter and left behind a book about battles."

So that's where I left it. Stupid. I never got to finish it.

"So believe what I say. The PA's battle barge cannot win any normal battle. They're heavily armed, but they have no supply chain. They are deep in enemy territory, in plain sight, with every hand against them. All they can do is fight until they run out of ammunition, and then be killed."

John nodded, puzzled. "Then why?"

"To get close enough to detonate their bomb. The only thing that makes sense is that they have a bomb so powerful that one explosion will destroy the city and the Starmen's ships and facilities, just as they claimed."

"Is such a thing possible?"

"In the Golden Age, such bombs were the great threat that influenced all other battle strategy. Two of those explosions ended a war that had consumed the whole world."

Jerry tried to pause and clear his head. Maybe it was just his own runaway fears. Had they claimed a nuclear bomb? Was it just his imagination?

"I don't know what kind of bomb they have, but it could also be poisonous. You and Sally have to get out of here."

"But...how can I leave..."

"John! We have to plan for the worst. A bomb from my time could easily burn this place to ashes and flatten it to the ground in an instant. Do you have a vehicle?"

"Yes, Sally's truck. She's driving over now."

"Then get in it and head south. If it's poisonous, the winds will cause it to drift to the north and east."

"Lord Jereomy, are you talking about 'radio poisoning'?"

"Radioactivity. Yes."

John looked troubled. "I need to warn my friends."

"You don't have time."

"But I can't leave them. Not if I can help."

Jerry knew exactly what he meant. "Okay. Do you have a phone tree?"

"I don't know what that is."

"You call one person, they pass the warning on to several others. Each of them warns more."

"The church does that."

"Then use it. Call them and give them the same warning. Don't wait. Don't pack anything. Just get out of town. Head south. Can you do that?"

He nodded, picking up the phone.

Jerry got the hand cart and started out.

The traffic was picking up, and the announcement to avoid panic wasn't working. Most cars were heading out of town.

I'm Lord Jereomy. Stop! He held out his hand with all the authority he could muster and pulled the cart through the traffic. Some slowed. Some swerved. And he made it through.

He had to kick the sign down, but even then, the cart wouldn't fit through the doorway. He carried the generator in, and then just tossed the rest of the supplies inside.

"Jerry!"

With panicked eyes, Sally was driving and Lil was shouting out the window of the little truck. Sally pulled the tiller hard to the side and drove her wheels up onto the grassy island. Lil was out the door.

He ran to meet her.

"Jerry! Is it a nuclear attack?"

"I don't know. But that's the way to bet."

"Do we run or stay?"

"I vote we stay with the box. Without us inside to turn it on, it'll be flattened like every other building. We'd be stuck in a radioactive fallout zone."

"Would it survive a nuclear blast, even active?"

It was a good question, with no hard evidence. But even radioactivity was subject to time.

She read his hesitation. "I'm with you, anyway. Do we take them?"

More than anyone else they'd met in their time journey, he felt friendship with John and Sally, and their parents before them. "We'll offer."

Lil and Sally hurriedly threw some clothes into the Doorway.

John saw them and came running. Dodging the traffic that was turning into a full fledged mass exodus, he was carrying books.

"Lord Jereomy! Take my book. Please take it to the future." He handed over his pride and joy, and the dictionary.

He took them. "John, do you and Sally want to come with us?"

Brother and sister exchanged befuddled glances. Their words dropped free of Golden Age and all Lil and Jerry could understand was their gestures.

John turned back. "No. I have to stay and write the next book."

Jerry took him into a big hug. "Then get out of town. Try to take a western road to get hills between you and the city, and don't be the first ones back if they say all is clear. The poisons can last for years."

Lil and Sally were exchanging their own goodbyes.

Only when Sally had wedged her truck back into the flow of escaping cars did Jerry grab Lil's hand and pull her into the copper room.

"How far?"

"I don't know, but use the fast setting. The higher the ratio, the safer we'd be from blast effects."

She turned the dial and flipped the switch. A whine of days started.

...

"Did it happen? Was there an explosion?"

"I just don't know. It would just have been a little click, if anything."

"Do we stop then? It's been years already."

But while they were debating, the whine stopped.

"Oh no."

Lil grabbed his hand. "Is it another global winter?"

"It's possible." He held his breath, waiting for the whine to return, like it did before. Seconds went by with no change.

Jerry looked around the room. "If a blast happened close to the room, it could have been tossed like a single dice. We'd have a one in six chance of landing right side up, unless someone turned us right side up later.

"Go grab the edge of that equipment rack, and be ready to duck into the corner if things start flying."

She nodded, "What about you?"

"I'll just hang onto the door latch. I have to be here to flip the switch."

He waited until she was in position.

"Ready?"

She nodded.

He flipped the switch and his stomach told him something was very wrong.

Year 1650

"Jerry!"

"Stay put."

At first, nothing seemed wrong. Nothing was tilted. Nothing was...

And then one of the chairs began floating up off the floor. It was a slow drift, and then when gold balls began peeking up from behind the bed, it was clear.

"Lil. We've lost our gravity. You have to move carefully."

"Can you turn it back on?"

He reached for the switch, then paused, the memory of a soldier in black struggling with all his might to pick up a tripod.

"I don't dare."

"Why?" Lil was hesitantly releasing her grip on the equipment rack. Her hair was drifting up into her face, and she swatted it back.

"It wouldn't get our gravity back, and it might cause problems. Give me time to think."

Lil's movements were having unintended side effects. Drifting a couple of feet above the floor, swinging her arms around, sent her into a slow spin, and her long skirt flying on its own path. Soon, she was just a tangle of bare legs and startlingly white panties and a dark blue skirt that was threatening to engulf her head like a giant shark.

"Jerry!"

He looked over the controls, just to make sure he hadn't left something in a dangerous position. Just to be safe, he turned both dials to the off position. A tumble against the wall had set them off on this journey in the first place.

"Hang on. Stop fighting it."

He pushed off the wall, and immediately bumped against a chair that had drifted up. Then, a set of clothes tossed into the room at the last minute snared his leg. By the time he reached her, he had been turned around and bumped into her backwards.

"Oof." He reached out and snagged her ankle at the same moment she grabbed his hair. They both hit the wall.

Jerry snagged the rack with one hand and with something stable to hold onto, Lil managed to climb around him until they were face to face. He held her with his free arm as both of them caught their breaths.

Lil's face was flushed and embarrassed. "Get that grin off your face."

"Why? I didn't see anything."

She slapped at her skirt again. "I have to change clothes, first thing."

He looked around at the psychotic fish aquarium that their cosy room had become. "I have to corral all the gold balls. There are exposed wires on the equipment rack that could get shorted by accident."

"What happened?"

He shrugged. "We lost gravity. That's all I know for now. But right now, we have to get order, or greater disasters could happen. I don't want to have the lights shorted out."

She shivered. "Right. What do we do?"

He looked her in the eyes. "Take off your skirt."

She bit her lip and then nodded. He tried to concentrate on how to get the gold under control, but it was difficult as she wriggled in his loose grip, unfastening her buttons and pulling the offending garment free.

"You can let me go now."

He liked the feel of her. "Are you sure?"

She flashed a slight smile. "Yes. As soon as I put a band on my hair, I'll be fine. Go get your balls under control."

He let her slip free, and she grabbed a floating chair on the way to her bags.

He sighed and pushed off one-handed towards the closest group of balls, sparkling as they drifted under the LED lights.

...

Lil wasted no time layering her gym shorts over her underwear and fixing her hair gymnastics style. Once she got her mind in the right frame, it was even fun to fly through the air, snagging things and putting them to right.

"Use the refrigerator," Jerry called when she began collecting the food supplies. It wasn't plugged in, but it was effectively a pantry with a door that stayed closed.

He was making big gold balls out of little ones by unfolding one to build a purse with a tail to hold others. The tail he wrapped around a lamp fixture to keep it from drifting.

Clothing could be bagged, and some of the new items were more immediately useful as straps to hold things together.

"Lil, do you have any string or twine?"

"I've got heavy thread, several spools of it."

"Good."

He began tying the bigger furniture into a web. It wouldn't keep their legs on the floor, but it would keep them roughly in place.

"Watch out for that!"

"Okay." She had accidentally kicked the chemical toilet. Luckily, all the chemicals were behind sealed valves and closed lids, but as she stopped it from spinning and eased it back to the floor level so Jerry could secure it, she wondered how they would deal with that problem when it arose. Maybe she shouldn't drink too much water for a while.

"Jerry, I'm going to cut some holes in the bedspread."

"Okay. Why?"

"I'll be able to secure it to the bed with straps, and hold all the covers, sheets and stuff in place."

Jerry drifted over to the doorway and tried to move the latch. It didn't budge.

"What are you doing?" she asked.

"I just had to test it. It seems like we are in space. But I didn't know if we were in vacuum or if we were in a pressurized space ship."

"Well?"

"The door won't budge. With a six by two and a half feet wide door...what's fifteen times fifteen times a hundred and forty-four?"

"Thirty some thousand."

"Right, fifteen or sixteen tons of air pressure holding it tightly closed. With the time circuit off, we're just lucky these walls are strong enough to keep the inside air pressure from rupturing a seam."

"So, no air outside?"

He nodded and drifted over to examine the electrical equipment.

. . .

A puff of air from the air recycling equipment sent a few light-weight objects flying. Some had escaped notice by floating quietly in between the furniture.

Lil noticed the change in the air and took in a deep breath. Almost immediately, it shut down again.

"What's wrong?"

"Nothing. I was just testing it. We'll have to ration the use of the air system until I can get more charge into the batteries." He flashed a blade. "We'd be sunk if you hadn't picked up this knife."

He uncoiled the extension cable and began cutting off the plugs.

"Will the generator work with our stuff?" she asked, as she snagged a loose sheet of paper out of the air. She tapped the wall with her foot to aim her back to where she'd bundled up the books.

"It should. It's direct current, so I'm bypassing the converter and wiring it directly to the battery bus. When I checked it with the volt meter, it looked like it was producing up to thirty volts, depending upon how fast I cranked."

"And that will keep us alive?"

"I think."

He didn't look her in the eye. She didn't know how to read that.

"Why haven't we turned the time accelerator back on?"

He paused and turned to face her. "It's risky. You remember that the tripod mounted gun was caught up into the time field when you flipped it on that one time. I think that anything metal that's in electrical contact with the skin of the copper room when we turn it on gets affected too.

"If we're in a space ship, strapped down to something metal, turning on the field could drag the whole spaceship into a time shift with us."

"And that would be bad?"

"That would make the pilot or the autopilot miss their destination. Our only hope is for someone to get us safely down to the ground again. We can't do anything to mess them up."

She nodded. "And you're sure we're in a spaceship?"

He gestured around the room. "No gravity. What other explanation is there?"

She looked down. "What if the Earth blew up?"

"No. Planets don't blow up. We won't ever see that happen, not if we crank up the dial and go a million years. They smash into things, or stars can boil them away, but they don't just blow up."

He sounded so confident. She nodded.

"Then what if that nuclear bomb in Canton knocked us up into space."

"Highly unlikely. I can imagine a bomb knocking a pebble into space, if conditions were just right. But not us. Not even if the battle barge docked real close to our position."

"So, space ship?"

He nodded. "A honking big space ship, bigger than anything we're used to, but it's the only thing I can imagine.

"And the only reason a space ship would take us into space is to relocate us to another planet. It would be an expensive operation, which makes us valuable. So, we need to be careful to not upset our only chance to survive this."

"So you think we can stay alive?"

He nodded, but his face wasn't full of confidence.

"What are you not telling me?"

He looked at the equipment rack. He sighed.

"If I can keep it charged, we have enough extra oxygen and enough of the chemicals to strip carbon dioxide for a few days—I don't know how many. The whine noise went away and we kept traveling into the future another five hundred years or so, right?"

"So we're not traveling faster than light. We're on a slow cruise. We are being shipped at the cheap rate. If the journey is already five hundred years in progress, the chances that it'll be finished in the next couple of days is nil.

"So if we turn on the time circuit, we could mess up the flight. If we don't, we run out of air."

...

Lil was tucked into bed, holding John's book and referring frequently to the translation dictionary, although it was almost as frustrating.

"Hey, did you know that we're Chinese?"

"Huh?" He was cranking the generator while tethered to a chair by strap of cotton cloth.

"Yes, according to this one legend, I was the daughter of the Emperor of China and we landed on the Pacific coast and crossed the Rocky Mountains on foot before discovering Canton. We were led to the city because its name was similar to a province of southern China."

"You're making sense of the book?" He paused, the sweat beading up in place on his skin.

"Pieces of it. John collected every legend he could find and wrote them all down. It's got a good index, so I'm reading the ones about me.

"Do you think he ever wrote the second book?"

"We may never know. Even if he did, it was centuries ago on a planet far behind us." He pulled off his shirt and used it to wipe at the sweat and went back to cranking the generator. The lights brightened slightly as the voltage came up.

Lil watched the muscles on his back, thinking about their future, or their lack of it.

"Keep your back turned. I'm changing clothes."

"Hmm."

. . .

She tapped on his shoulder. He looked and said, "What in the world?"

She pointed to the generator. "It's my turn. Show me how to work this."

He adjusted the stirrup for her shorter leg and fit the strap around her waist.

"The outfit is...nice."

"You mean it makes me look like a porn star." She began cranking.

"Hmm. Maybe. Perhaps a dominatrix."

"It's actually a Peterson fancy dress. 'Petersons' are what Sally calls their people." She didn't really need his hand on her shoulder keeping her in place, but she wasn't going to mention it.

"Sally says that her people feel constrained by ordinary clothing. 'Everybody has hair', she says, 'but we just have finer hair, and more of it.' So when Petersons get together for exclusive events, the girls tend to wear outfits that really display their pelts to advantage. Thus outfits like this that are just straps of cloth.

"When I saw how much you were sweating, I thought this would be the appropriate outfit to wear while working."

"Uh huh." He let go of her shoulder and drifted a few inches away. Nothing else seemed to demand his attention. His eyes were all on her.

"Did you know Sally had a crush on you?" she asked with a grin.

"No. Did she?"

"Yes, when she was little and you taught them math at her house, she thought you were the most wonderful guy she'd ever seen."

He chuckled.

"And when she was a teenager, she'd have fantasies about you, and what wonderful furry little children you and she would have."

"You're making that one up!"

"No. It's true. You didn't see her blush while we were measuring you? I could see it even under her fur."

"Well, I do say that I thought her mother was particularly striking."

Lil reached out and punched him.

"Hey! What did I do?" he said as he tumbled slowly across the room.

. . .

Jerry wrinkled his nose. His arms, which had been drifting as he dozed off under the sheets encountered Lil, floating just over the bed, holding a thread in her hand. He pulled her close. "Stop that."

She tossed the thread aside. "You just looked so inviting there, with your arms stretched out like that."

He kissed her, and taking advantage of the Peterson dress, he moved his fingers under one of the strategic straps. She didn't struggle.

"Jerry?"

"Um. Yes?" He kissed her again.

"What do you think about sex before marriage?"

Strangely, that didn't set off any alarm bells in his head.

"You mean right now? Trapped in airless space, with no future consequences to worry about?" It actually felt good to say it. He kissed her again.

She had a little frown, but returned the kisses eagerly.

"No. I mean theoretically." She put her arm around his neck and hugged herself tightly to his chest. Her head was beside his, whispering into the pillow.

"Let's just assume we'll live. You'll figure something out, or magic will happen. Should I crawl under the sheets with you?"

"You're stacking the deck. You know I want to."

He could feel every word as she whispered beside his ear. "I know. But what do you *think*?"

He stared past her hair at the ceiling above. It was unfair. It was hard.

"Lil. If I get carried away. I won't find it hard to forgive myself. I've come close before. I was close a few seconds ago."

"But?"

"But you told me to think." He took a deep breath. "And I think we need to hold on. All the rules are gone. All the laws are obsoleted. Parents, preachers, judging eyes of friends and relatives. It's all gone. All we have left of who we are and what we believe about what is right and wrong are right here." He tapped her head, and then his.

"If it was right to keep my...hands out of your pants a few days ago when we were sneaking off to study together, then it's right even now."

He twisted to face her, and was concerned to see her eyes.

"You're crying?" He caressed her face and tried to brush at tears that had no down to tell them where to flow. "I'm sorry."

"No. It's okay. It's all right. You think, somehow, that we will live." She smiled. "You wouldn't fight so hard otherwise. You'd lie and make me feel better."

And she was right. There was either something he was missing, or else he'd just have to bite the bullet and risk the time field. But somehow, they would live. They'd have to.

"Lil? Will you marry me?"

"Yes, silly. Did you ever think otherwise? I've been dating you for nearly a couple of thousand years!"

. . .

He cranked the generator, watching Lil bounce from the bed to the ceiling, doing a half flip in the process and pushing off with her feet to do another half flip to land on the bed. She was certainly burning off some of the nervous energy they'd built up in an enthusiastic and frustrating make-out session. She'd also changed back to her gym clothes, promising to reserve the Peterson dress for after their marriage.

Up she went, bouncing so hard on the ceiling that he worried about the strength of the copper plates. Even the tied-down furniture bounced with her.

He frowned. That was strange. He looked at the table lifting and settling in sympathy with her zero-gravity trampoline activity.

"Lil! Stop."

She looked his way and landed on her back against the mattress and then drifted as it tossed her back up.

"Sorry."

"No. It's not that. I just noticed something."

"The way my breasts are so perky in zero-gravity?"

"No! Yes, well I did, but that's not it."

"The furniture, everything in the room is bouncing with you when you hit the mattress or the ceiling. So. That means you are pushing the whole room."

She tapped the wall and drifted back his way. "Put it together for me. I'm not seeing it."

"If...if you're moving the room, then it means that the room is not strapped down to a space ship hundreds of times more massive than it is."

"No space ship? I thought you proved there was?"

"Maybe. Can you do that back flip thing between this wall and that one?" He pointed to the two side walls which had enough flat unencumbered space.

"Okay." She pushed off his hand and reached the wall. "Gym class was never like this." She put her legs 'under' her and shoved off. The first flip was slightly off, but quickly, she got the rhythm.

His eyes watched everything.

"Okay, now I want you to go back and do the same thing you did before, ceiling to mattress."

As he untangled himself from the generator and drifted over to the time controls, she shifted her angles and began bouncing up and down.

He watched carefully through several cycles and then just at the right instant, shortly after her feet left the mattress, he flipped the switch.

"Okay, you can stop."

She rose to the ceiling and this time, she killed her motion slowly, rather than bouncing.

"Something's different."

He nodded. All over the room, furniture, the generator, and his fiancee were settling slowly towards the floor.

"What did you do?"

"We are in a space ship. But instead of being clamped into a fixed location, we appear to be secured by a web of elastic cords. Every time you hit a wall or floor or ceiling, everything moved the opposite direction, for just an instant, until the wall was restored to its position by the cords."

He pointed to the controls. "I turned on the time field and it appears that I was able to freeze the rebound, just as we have been freezing the effect of gravity before."

She chuckled. "I even know that one. We had it in physics class not a month ago. Einstein's Principle of Equivalence. A change of velocity is no different from gravity."

"I guess so. Who knows if it will last, but it gives us a fraction of a gravity. Enough to put the table legs on the floor."

"Ah, Jerry?"

"Yes?"

"Would the toilet work now?"

He looked skeptical. "You'd have to be very careful. I'd do it only in an emergency."

"Oh, it is. It is."

He turned his back. "Okay, but have a cleanup towel handy."

A minute or so later, she said, "It worked. But I think we need to run the air recycler again."

He'd noticed.

...

They strapped a chair next to the control switch and he cranked the generator while she jumped them through time in roughly ten year leaps.

Their faux gravity went away, but if they needed it again, Lil could do her bouncing trick to restore it.

"How long do we keep doing this?"

"As long as we need to. If the air system gives out, we'll jump faster, but I don't want to go past the calibrated point if we don't have to. I'd hate do discover that we started jumping a million years at a time and not notice until humanity was extinct."

"We could be Adam and Eve."

"Probably on a dead planet. No. Play it cautious."

After a more than three hundred years, the furniture all dropped with a thud.

"We're down. Jump us twenty more years."

Lil did so, and unstrapped herself from the chair. Jerry set the generator aside and turned off the air system.

Year 2005

"Did you hear a whine?"

"No. Did you?"

He shook his head.

Well, one thing at a time.

"My arms ache." He tested his legs. "How does the gravity feel to you?"

She stepped a few paces. "I need to put the bra back on, but it feels normal. I can't tell."

He nodded. "Close to Earth normal if the zero-gravity hasn't messed with our muscles."

He walked around to where he'd stashed his shirt. "Watch out for the threads. Don't trip."

She nodded, having almost made his warning redundant.

"I'm taking a peek outdoors."

He moved slowly, carefully. Logic indicated they were on an advanced world. But the lack of the time whine was disturbing. All kinds of fatal possibilities flashed through his head, from automated warning devices, through poisonous atmosphere, to deadly diseases, just waiting for them.

The door latch moved easily, opening the seal. There was a whoosh for a fraction of a second as the higher air pressure outside equalized with what they had inside.

Chemical smell. Faint. He opened the door a crack.

They were inside a large room. At least there was no gold foil. He opened it wider. Distant footsteps echoed, giving him a sense of the size of the place. He eased outside.

No alarms, and the footsteps receded in the distance.

The copper room was on a slightly elevated platform, just a couple of inches above a floor that looked like marble.

A minute later he came back inside and closed and latched the door. "Well?"

"Have you ever been to the Smithsonian or any other large museum?"

"Not really. Just local ones."

"I think we're in the Grandaddy of all museums. Imagine a room that stretches for miles, lined with exhibits. None of them with labels or signs, but all in great shape, and all big things. We aren't the biggest exhibit by a long shot. It's probably night, and I don't think the temperature varies, so that's why we didn't hear the whine. I also saw robots, floor sweepers."

"So what do we do now?"

He stretched out on the bed beside her and put his hands behind his head.

"I think I'd like to wander around, but maybe during normal hours so I won't get tagged as a thief. For now, we have fresh air, and the batteries are charged up to 60%. I think I'll take a break."

"How about lunch? Something more elaborate than bread?"

"Sounds great. In a minute."

After a few kisses, Lil got to her feet. Silently, Jerry rolled off the bed and grabbed her with his hand across her mouth.

Frozen together, they listened as faint outside footsteps grew louder and then paused outside the door.

Then the steps went on their way.

"A night guard," he whispered.

Jerry went to the dial and froze the outside world.

"Let's at least be able to eat in peace."

...

Lil noted the time on her cell phone and wrote it down on the sheet of paper. "Thirty-seven minutes on the dot. I don't think this guard actually tugged on the door. I think he just tapped it with his finger." She turned off the cell phone. "My calendar appears to be a couple of millennia off."

"Hmm."

She looked back at the bed. His eyes moved up to look at hers and he smiled.

She tugged at her gym shorts. "If you don't get your mind back in the game, I'm going to change into the white dress."

"I'll help."

She gave him a severe look.

He put up his palm in surrender. "Sorry. I was just distracted."

"Look." She glared down at him. "I know what's going on. I get... daydreams too. But con-sum-a-tion ain't gonna happen until we get ourselves a wedding, and that's not going to happen in here. Your rules!"

He nodded and stood up. He put his arms around her.

"Night guards are on a thirty-seven minute rotation, which probably means their clocks are on a different scale. Probably because their day/night period has changed. We aren't Earth-centric anymore. No alarm was sounded when I went outside, so they probably don't have constant visual scanners. This is a hall of huge exhibits, so they aren't concerned about people putting something valuable in their pocket and walking out. Since they check the door, they probably are thinking about thieves who could hide inside and then rob some other wing of the place.

"That will be our biggest problem. We can't leave the door un-latched. Guards or visitors will be testing it all the time. So one of us will have to stay inside at all times." He kissed the top of her head.

She pulled out of his arms. "We will trade off! I'm not staying in here all the time while you go off and have all the fun." She took a couple of steps and looked back at where he stood.

"And please, put your shirt back on. It's distracting."

...

Jerry had put on his frowny face when she'd won the coin toss. She liked having him always around to take care of her, but she had to be firm and keep him in his place at times.

Lil poked her head out, hearing the echoing voices off the high ceiling. No one was in direct line of sight, so she slipped out and moved quickly around the copper walls. The door closed with just the faintest of clicks.

Hidden from the tour group passing by she straightened the drape of her white dress and tried to correct any stray lock of hair by feel.

I left my mirror inside.

But she wouldn't go back in to retrieve it. The idea had been to keep her possessions to a minimum. The fewer the anachronisms, the less likely they'd attract attention. And there was hardly a time period in history where the white dress wouldn't have been acceptable.

She patted the bulge in her sash that contained her phone. They needed photos of their surroundings and she'd already proved she could handle that job. Thirty minutes, and she'd be back with enough info so that they could form a plan.

From where she hid, she could see a half dozen of the other exhibits, and a big expanse of the wall. Jerry had mentioned that there were no signs, and he was right. There should have been labels all over the place.

The nearest exhibit appeared to be a pile of rocks, but someone thought it was important. Beyond it was...a space ship? Maybe a sculpture of one? It was curvy and artistic rather than utilitarian. In the distance, a stone statue looked like one of those heads from Easter Island, but it was easily forty feet high, and highlighted just how big this room was.

She peered around the corner and got a good look at the nearest tour group. Two girls whispering together saw her and pointed. She ducked back out of sight, but there came an authoritarian voice calling.

It probably wouldn't hurt to blend in with the crowd. She came around the corner and the lady in the front of the group with the blue sash said something to her.

"Sorry. I just got mixed up." Lil did her best little lost girl imitation, staring at her shoes with her hands folded together. It had worked a number of times when she'd been caught in the hallway when she should have been in study hall, and it worked again.

The tour guide looked frustrated. She dug out a little pouch from her sash and handed it to her with firm instructions, from the tone of her voice.

Lil nodded and opened the pouch. The guide went back to her lecture, pointing at a large metal hoop standing vertical, just opposite their copper room. The group turned almost as one, even though individually they looked as different as could be. *Is that blue hair natural, or colored?*

Inside the pouch was a simple pair of frameless goggles. Wraparound colorless lenses extended into their own earpieces. She put them on, and blinked.

Oh.

. . .

Jerry closed the door and latched it with misgivings. Yes, it wasn't fair that he got to go out first all the time, but they were in a completely new environment. Who know what hazards there were?

At least it appeared to be a civilized and urban setting. One would hope that a stranger would be able to get by without too much immediate danger.

They had both charged their cell phones, and he checked his time. Thirty minutes and she'd be back. He wished there was a way to set his phone's clock. It was designed to pull accurate time from the cell phone towers, but those were long gone. Lil's phone had never totally gone dead, so it was still bravely counting the seconds, still thinking it was back in the 21st Century. His battery had dropped below the critical point and when he recharged it, the clock had reset itself to a manufacture's date or something. It was totally different from Lil's. As a time piece, it was only good as a personal stop watch. His lap-top was in much better shape, and its clock was a reasonably faithful counter of the time it had spent inside the copper room. Of course, that wasn't his personal time. Nor was his time the same as Lil's. The whole idea of the 'real' time was just nonsense.

But some time by himself had its advantages. Before she came tap-tap-tapping on the door, he wanted to change and clean up. Lil was picky about things like that. And now that he had a replacement set of clothes, it was a good time to try them out.

Sally and Lil had picked out a matching shirt and slacks in some beige color. It didn't match his shoes at all, but that couldn't be helped. He hurriedly sponged off and tried them on. It felt different. But it did smell clean.

...

Ten minutes until Lil was due back, he sat by the door, his hand on the latch, ready to pull her in, the instant she was back.

Five 'til, he daydreamed of grabbing a handful of white. He could be more impulsive with a fully clad Lil. He had to be cautious when she was in her gym outfit, and positively restrained in that Peterson 'dress'. His arms ached in anticipation.

Time was up. Where was she? Had she run into trouble?

Only five minutes late. Of course, something like this couldn't be on an exact deadline. She might not even be able to check her cell phone clock.

Fifteen minutes late. He shouldn't worry. He was late hours past his thirty minute scouting expedition into the walled version of Canton. But maybe he should find a way to look out for her.

After risking a couple of quick looks, he had to quickly close and latch the door when one of the touring groups came up close to touch the walls and test the door.

...

I can't go looking for her. The doorway would be compromised in minutes, day or night. I have to find a way.

Only two things kept the door closed, the inside latch, or a time field. There was no way to manipulate the latch by remote control.

Something had happened to Lil, and there was no way for her to get in touch with him. He had to find a way to go hunt for her.

...

He had barely considered it before, but now, holding the knife in his hand, he felt the enormity of what he was thinking of doing.

Lil had been gone for four hours. He had to do something.

Uncle Greg had mentioned adding a timer circuit to the controls. It had to be possible. He just had to figure out how.

Carefully, he used the tip of the knife blade to loosen the tamper resistant screws that held the time control box together. It was the wrong tool for the job, but he had nothing better. The next closest tool was the key to his car, and it was probably too fat to fit into the cavity.

With a tiny snap, the screw began to turn. Quarter turn at a time, he loosened each of the five screws. After too many contortions, the case opened along the seam. Two of the screws dropped to the floor, and he had to stop everything to locate them. He didn't know if they were critical, but he couldn't chance it.

Seven hours after Lil's deadline, he had a crude sketch of the wiring. The dials weren't even electrical. They moved some kind of solenoids in and out of the real mechanism. The on/off switch also just activated an electromagnet that pulled a metal slug in and out of the metal time circuit device. An entirely different circuit was on all the time, fed directly from the battery wires that crossed over from the equipment rack underneath the baseboard trim.

So, if the dials were set properly manually, could he turn the system on directly by wire, rather than by flipping a switch? How much power did the solenoid take?

...

Two hours later, he had a system that worked.

The only 'timer' that he had was his laptop. He had learned some time ago through painful experience that while his cell phone could be charged from the laptop's USB port, when the laptop went to sleep, so did the power to the USB cable.

As part of the laptop's energy saver system, he could order the computer to go to sleep after a short interval of inactivity. It also had the capability to wake itself up.

It took some hacking, locating the correct settings and modifying them to work faster than the factory settings of sleep after five minutes and wake once a day. He got it down to sleep after one minute, and then wake up at any interval longer than one minute.

Carefully, he set it running.

The laptop woke. The USB cable had four wires, two for data and two for power. The voltmeter told him which ones were power. He cut and spliced into the solenoid control, bypassing the time circuit's on/off switch. When the laptop was awake, so was the time circuit. One minute later the laptop went to sleep, and the time circuit turned off.

If I set it to sixty times normal, then I can exit the door, close it behind me, and let the copper room freeze for an hour. It will unfreeze itself for one minute, and then repeat.

He didn't like it that the window that the door could be opened by any stray hand was a whole minute long. Unattended, that was long enough for the door to be discovered by accident. But it was the best he could do with the tools at hand.

He made sure that the laptop was charged, and plugged into the main battery system.

Maybe it would be better to freeze it for several hours, or a day? But that would make it harder to get back in when he needed to.

He settled on three hours.

The final piece of the puzzle required him to break one of the chairs. With an L-shaped lever, weighted by nearly fifty pounds of books, and suspended from the door frame, the iron door would remain shut, tightly enough for the electrical seal in spite of the fact that the latching lever was left open.

Jerry ran the operation several cycles, until he was sure that it was reliable.

He didn't say it out loud to himself, but he knew the risk he took. He and Lil could be stranded in this time forever if one thing failed and the room never unlocked itself. It would rocket towards the future leaving them behind until the the electrical system finally died, in the altered time stream.

. . .

Outside it was the dimmed lights and quiet halls. Lil had been gone all day long.

I have to wait until the time she left—give her a full day. But if she's not back by then, I'm going to try to find her myself.

He counted hours in his head. There was time for a little sleep. If he could.

. . .

The shirt from Sally's store reminded him of one he saw his pharmacist wearing a couple of personal months ago. He checked the time and slipped his phone into one of the low shirt pockets. Holding a clipboard with a dozen blank pages and topped with a horribly dense page of instructions for applying for an athletic scholarship, enough to confuse anyone, no matter what time period you were from, he stepped outside and closed the door gently behind him. He stepped to the side and waited, watching. When the color shifted slightly, he sighed.

The first of the tour groups were almost close enough to make out the individuals. He had to decide what to do.

It was almost like a parade, except instead of bands and floats passing by, there were groups of tourists and scholars. From what he could see, about half of the groups were on foot, but there were others that seemed to be riding a low platform, and still others that looked like open air tour busses. The corridors were a constant babble of voices.

He had to be independent, and for a place like this, that meant people had to think he was a security guard or a scholar. He held his clipboard at ready and started walking down the aisle off to the side and opposite the flow of traffic.

He rarely met the eyes of the people he passed. A girl in a white dress or with Lil's hair color would attract his closer look, but even when people spoke to him, he tried to keep his eyes on his clipboard and ignore them.

I'm busy. I don't have time to talk.

Stay in the pose. If he could make himself believe it, then so would they.

But as he passed by the first ten people, and then the first hundred, and the first thousand, the size of the place began to bear down on him. He marked the number of cross corridors on his clipboard, trying to keep track of where he was.

He'd described his first impression as like the Smithsonian. But that was just from a quick glimpse out the door. This was more like a whole city!

After he walked an hour, it was plain that these people hadn't come from outside. He stopped at a corridor that led to wide open spaces that appeared to be living areas filled with stores and seating areas and people wandering about.

Should I go there? He'd planned to find the entrance to the museum, but maybe there wasn't one. Was this place a massive building, or a city underground? It was well lit, but the lighting came from uniform panels high along the walls, not from skylights.

We didn't have the time whine. So maybe there's no day/night temperature difference.

Lil was somewhere, but the population—just from what he'd seen thus far—was many thousands. It could be much, much more. And how, other than wandering the crowds and checking each face, could he ever find her?

I can't lose you.

A queasiness in his stomach had been growing as the size of his task bore down on him.

There was a tap on his shoulder. He spun around.

A man wearing a gray coat that went down to his knees smiled and asked him something.

"Sorry. I was distracted. I may have lost my way."

He gestured with the clipboard, hinting at some important task he was doing.

The man looked puzzled. He tapped a pair of goggles that Jerry hadn't even realized the man was wearing. They were transparent and showed no surface glare.

"Sorry? I don't understand."

The man looked off into the distance and appeared to be talking to the air. He patted Jerry on the shoulder again.

He could do nothing but shrug. If this guy had called the cops, or was a cop, there was nowhere to run, not in a place this enclosed and this organized.

Out of the 'resident' corridor, a single figure came zipping up, standing on a personal platform about three feet wide, riding a couple of inches above the floor like a business professional's version of Silver Surfer's board.

It was a female, looking very much like a member of Ason's variety. She was tall and very thin, but dressed in a slacks and jacket, not overly bundled up. Like Ason, she was hairless, but Jerry had no doubt she was human and female.

She stepped off the platform as it smoothly slowed to a stop. She exchanged a couple of words with the man in gray, and he turned to go.

Jerry shrugged when she spoke to him. She smiled and handed him a package, a pair of goggles in a pouch.

He put them on, as if they were perfectly normal.

But they were more than glasses. Rows of text appeared before him in the air, probably projected into his eyes by the goggles. Only one item in the third column made any sense.

PRE-EXPANSION ENGLISH.

Almost as soon as he read those words, the display cleared and a set of questions appeared.

In his ears, he heard, "Is that better now?"

It plainly came from the lady.

He nodded. "Yes. I'm sorry to have caused you trouble."

She smiled. "People lose their goggles all the time. Hopefully when you enter your numbers, your customization will all come back. If it doesn't, just contact Services and we'll help you out. Can you find your way now?"

"Yes, probably."

"I'd recommend taking the time to get it configured, or the advertisements will nag you to death. Bye now."

She stepped back on her platform and it whisked her away.

A universal translator. Wonderful. He took a deep breath and let his arms relax at his side.

A great worry vanished. The farther he got from his home time, the more headaches the language shift had been. This gadget was his new first priority. He had to puzzle out its features or he'd be nothing but a lost child in this place.

As he looked over toward the corridor, all the blank walls he'd seen were now covered in text. A sign advertising "Great Pasta, Comfortable Seating" pointed down into the maze.

Sounds good.

. . .

The questions were simple, to begin with. His name, his birth date, planet and location. The goggles were excellent at translating his low mumbles into text. And when it entered 'Jeromy Harris' as his name, it understood when he stared at his first name and said, "Change spelling to J-E-R-E-O-M-Y."

It didn't bobble an instant when he entered his correct birthdate. It made no judgement call when someone claimed to be over 2000 years old.

He'd waffled for a few minutes over whether he should enter his correct information or not. But it seemed to him that he shouldn't get in a habit of lying in a place like this. He was okay with letting people assume incorrect things, but in the news of his home era, there were constant stories of people who had been caught at lies, and often the penalties for fraud were much greater than for the secret they were trying to hide.

The museum seemed wired to the extreme. A place like that would put a priority on accuracy, and just might make the deceiver suffer for the attempt.

His personal biometrics seemed to be filling out on their own. Somehow, either the goggles or spy cameras he couldn't see had determined his correct height, weight, eye-color, sex and had marked him as Human-009. Something had even provided a wallet-shot of his face.

Human-009. Does that mean there are non-humans wearing the goggles? And just how many variants are there that there needs to be three digits for the classes?

When it asked "Bonding status?" he answered, "Engaged." The word appeared and then winked out to be replaced with UNKNOWN.

Perhaps it didn't translate correctly. PRE-EXPANSION ENGLISH seemed to be pretty close to John's Golden Age English, but that could still refer to a period spanning hundreds of years.

As he located a comfortable table and put down his clipboard, a new set of questions appeared.

"Bank Account ID:"

He'd just have to skip that one. Even if his Missouri Bank of America savings account meant anything to the goggle's system, he'd never memorized the number. It was on his laptop somewhere. That was what computers were for.

...

Mary Montgomery stared across the table at her, twirling the albino-white lock of hair that was draped to show off her high-peaked ear.

Lil looked away from the mass of humanity that swirled past the residence and asked, "Yes?"

"Are you going to spend the whole day sitting out here?"

She glanced back at the crowd, always afraid that she would miss him. "Jerry will come for me eventually. I keep looking for him."

Mary chuckled, "You say you don't have his number, and you don't know where he is. Honey, you're just out of luck."

Lil's hands were always moving, clenching, fussing with her dress, pushing her hair back. "If I just had kept track of the route! I could go back and find it."

"That exhibit you say is yours?"

"Right."

"But you don't remember its catalog name?"

She shrugged. "I never named it. We just called it the copper room, but other people had names for it. It was quite legendary—The Doorway to Heaven."

"Did you search for that?"

Lil nodded, the advertisements were all for brothels, and one place that may have been a restaurant. "There was nothing that matched."

Mary adjusted her goggles slightly. "I wish I could say I remembered when you joined our group, but I was paying more attention to Kell than I was to the exhibits. The perils of a co-ed study group."

"I'm just grateful you put me up for the night."

"No problem. But you said you found your bank account?"

Lil laughed. "Yes, isn't that amazing? Two thousand years old, and closed out when I went missing, but the records floated around in ancient archives and must have been excavated, even after civilization collapsed at least twice. But the number survived, and this system accepted it. No cash, but it recognized me as the owner."

"Lil, if you're still amazed at the banking system, then you *must* be from someplace else. That's first session economics. Banking survives, if nothing else does. If a planet ever reneges on its banking obligations, then the ships don't come anymore.

"And I don't know about your claim of two thousand years, but my father spent two hundred years in transit from his home planet and his bank records were good as gold. It's just a fact of life when star travel takes so long."

Lil pointed, "But you said you were from another planet, Jen-9? How old does that make you?"

Mary waved her hand. "That's different. This star, Jen, has a dozen planets where people live. Well, some of them are moons, but that's beside the point. Planet to planet travel is boring, but it's over within a few weeks. Star to star trips are the big ones, where you say goodbye to your friends and relatives and never come back."

Lil felt a rush of pain. She'd put that loss on the back burner. Something to think about when she and Jerry were safe and settled. The face of her mother and father, and her little sister, the kids she'd grown up with. Favorite teachers and even friendly rivals crashed through her memory with a suddenness that left her gasping.

"What's wrong, Honey?"

"Nothing. Just...nothing. I'm okay."

Mary took her hand. "I know you're lying now. And it's okay. I'll stop pestering you."

Lil salvaged a smile. "You take my stories without a qualm, and now I'm lying?"

Mary tilted her head, considering.

"Okay. You gave me the tale of your sweetheart who saved the world."

"More than once."

"Yes, more than once. So I'll tell you why my mother finally gave in and let me spend an academic season all by myself here at the Museum of Humanity."

...

"Museum recruiters come visit all the schools and sanctuaries every year, pushing the idea that a visit to the Mother Hub, as we like to call it, is a necessary part of any child's education. The fact that all of our teachers and most of our parents had come here when they were young certainly makes it more likely that parents will save up the money and make it happen.

"Mom kept holding off. There was a school tour group that went a couple of years ago, but she didn't like the idea of me spending all that time with all those boys. 'Chaperones can be tricked,' she said. 'And boys can't be trusted.'

"Well, when I managed to get a Museum representative to come by the house and talk to her, the rep gave her the secret info that finally pushed Mom to let me come.

"It was the goggles."

Lil frowned. She tapped the weightless and nearly invisible lens with her fingernail. "These?"

"Yes. The rep explained that she understood how girls on their own needed a little edge when they were becoming women and were faced with a lot of attractive young men. You see, there's a secret in the settings. Now follow my instructions. Go to the halo settings."

Mary stepped her through the menus. Lil followed along, stepping down into the maze that controlled how the goggles showed the world to her. Lil had already noticed the halos, faint colored highlighting that surrounded the heads of other people who wore goggles. It told her at a glance who were students and who were teachers or security guards. It also let her know who had their translator software running so she could speak and be understood.

"Now go to the Special Functions menu and turn on Stress Analysis."

"Okay. I did."

"Now look at me."

Lil noticed a slight edge at the limits of her halo. It shifted and flickered.

"Now, I knew what was going on. My mother had come here, at about my age. She also came right back and married my father. She never talked about it, but I could read a calendar as well as anyone. She was probably already pregnant with me when she came home."

Mary looked carefully at Lil. "Now what did you see in the halo?"

"Um. There were...flares, I guess you'd call them. Stronger flickers at different times as you talked."

"Did you notice when they occurred?"

"Right at the last."

Mary smiled and nodded. "Right. Because that last part was a lie. She didn't come home pregnant. I just wanted to show you how the halo works."

"So, this can act as a lie detector?"

"Right. Mom was overjoyed that I would have a way to tell if a boy was just telling me a sweet tale, or if he was telling the truth. That's what gave her enough peace of mind to let me come here."

"And you were using it to see if I was lying to you?"

"I always have it turned on. Habit. I don't advertise the fact, but it's too useful to do without. Plus, you never know who else has that setting turned on. Just telling the truth is easier."

Lil noticed a slight flicker, but let it pass.

"So, what do you really think, about Jerry and me."

Mary shook her head. "I think you've put a golden glow around this guy and he'll probably let you down. You're going to need to get you a job, a room, and a new boyfriend."

Lil frowned. "I'm sorry I'm such a leech. I'll find a way to pay you back."

Mary shook her head. "That's not the point. You haven't cost me a thing sleeping on my couch and sharing my food points. That's not what I was saying. I just think guys tell you what you want to hear. They don't even think they're lying. They just want to get close to you, real close, and they say whatever it takes."

Lil felt a gentle glow inside her. Maybe it was a 'golden glow', but that didn't matter. "Jerry will find me. But I will need money. Do you think I could use this ancient bank account?"

"If the goggles recognize it, then sure."

Lil reached behind her head and unwound the braid. "Do you think I could sell this?" She held out her home-made hair band.

"I mean, is gold valuable in this time? I'll need money, if for no other reason than to schedule a tour back through the hallway to find my copper room."

Mary leaned forward, "Gold, yeah!" She took it and felt it. "Where did you get it?"

"I peeled the gold foil off a holy shrine dedicated to me."

Mary looked at her skeptically. "And when did you do this?"

Lil thought back. "Hmm. I lose track. Several centuries at least. More than a thousand years ago."

Mary nodded. "It's exasperating. You tell me unbelievable things, and I have to believe you. Well, if no one is coming to claim it, and you didn't steal it from any of the museum pieces, then it's probably okay."

"The museum probably never even knew about the gold. It was before their time."

After Mary did a little cost comparison using her goggles, she named a price and bought it herself. With nothing more than a mumble and a little staring into space, funds were transferred into Lil's account. Almost instantly, the advertisements on the walls grew brighter and more densely packed.

· · ·

With the goggles providing many of the same features Jerry expected from his laptop, it was frustrating to find the places where it fell short.

At the beginning, he quickly located his position on a map of the museum. Expanding the range and using the notes from his clipboard he identified the position of the copper room.

"I928734: Hollow metal room with door. Historical/religious artifact from G42-3."

Unfortunately more info than that was secured behind a paywall. This grand museum was no free banquet. It was pay as you go all the way. Even the goggles, although they were freely given, were mainly a way to beam advertisements into your brain. If you had a bank account, you could pay to turn them off.

As it was, he couldn't even pull up a picture of I928734 without paying for the next level of information.

Searching for Lil, under the assumption that she also had goggles and was somehow in the system, came up empty. Searching for people was off limits for no obvious reason.

"Crazy system."

A female voice caused him to turn his head. "You're a newcomer aren't you?"

She was a black...angel. That was his first impression. Skin, hair, and clothes were all deep black, with a reflective, almost metallic look. Her hair and the top of her shoulders and arms were trimmed in what looked at first like black feathers.

"Ah. Sorry. I was just trying to understand the goggles."

She moved and the 'feathers' rippled. It was probably fur rather than feathers. "I knew it." She laughed. "I see new guys all the time, sitting for hours, staring into space, deep into the data...and totally ignoring me."

Jerry shook his head and smiled. "I shouldn't have done that. Never ignore a beautiful girl. I must say, you are very...striking. Ultraviolet sun?"

She smiled, and while her teeth weren't black, they did show up like polished walnut. "And smart too. I get lines like, 'If they turn out the lights, do you vanish altogether.'

"Yes, I'm from Sessi-5. And I'm not looking forward to going back."

"Oh?" He knew a leading statement when he heard it. "Why is that?"

She shrugged. "It's a long trip. I was asleep sixty-five years getting here and it'll take at least that long getting back. I'll have a good job in the government when I get there, but everyone I know will be dead."

"I understand."

Black on black eyes stared at him in sympathy. "You have a long trip too?"

"You'd never believe me if I told you."

She moved over to his table and sat beside him. "I've been here a while and know all the tricks." She put her hand on his arm and smiled. "Let me help you out."

...

Lil stared at the spreadsheet of new arrivals to the museum, hanging in space in front of her like a curtain. ID number, arrival date, public tags and access status—not a name in the place, except for a few who had filled out their tags with names. And only a few of them had been brave enough to turn on public access.

"That's not how it's done," said Kell, who had dropped by to chat with Mary. He was plainly the same variety of human that Mary was, like an albino elf, and Lil suspected they had a history. That lie-detector halo showed more than just lies. It showed 'chemistry'.

He explained, "If you're public, your call flag will start bouncing and never stop, and all the calls will be from strangers wanting to sell you something. You stay private and authorize the people you meet in person."

"Like me," Mary purred.

Kell turned his attention back to her. "Like those special people you meet. Nice hair style, by the way."

Mary made her apologies. "Sorry to leave you to your own devices, but Kell and I have some studying to do." The halo said differently.

He glanced her way, "Later."

Lil shook her head as they walked off together. She muttered, "Is this place the educational center of the universe, or the dating center?"

Her goggles presented her with some statistics. Lil's jaw dropped. *No wonder this place is so popular.*

She dismissed the list of marriages, the numbers of residence changes, and pregnancies as the walls began filling up with advertisements for romantic date spots, pre-natal care, two-person residences, and the like.

"Wait a second. Replace that last set of advertisements."

She stared at ads on the walls and selected one.

. . .

"I need a bank account."

Nerib from Sessi-5 asked, "How could you even be here without a bank account?"

"It's a long story. But every time I try to dig deeper into the data, it's the same thing—please enter your bank id to gain access."

"So...you don't have any money?"

"Not in this database. I have resources, just not connected to this maze. And I can't get back to my other computer until I can find the way with this one."

"Well, I guess you could open a new account, and then merge it with your old one when you locate it."

Jerry nodded. "That would probably be best. Thanks."

She watched him grimace and flick his eyes back and forth, as if he were somewhere else, and not shoulder to shoulder at the table with her.

"Jeromy, would you do me a favor?"

"What's that?" He paused his goggle work and gave her his full attention.

She reached into her belt pouch and with a knowing smile, pulled out a small gray metallic cup. She set it on the table and added water from the carafe. "Take a sip, for me."

He looked at it with caution. "Ah, what is it?"

Her smile dropped. "You don't know?"

"No. Sorry."

She sighed. "And I thought I came from a backwater planet."

She held up the cup. "It takes a DNA sample from your saliva as you sip. That's all."

He frowned. "I guess that's all right." He took the little cup and sipped a bit of the water. She took it from him and stared at the sides of the cup. In a matter of a few seconds, a brightly colored pattern, like a dense bar code, appeared on metal.

Nerib sighed. "Oh, well, it was a long shot."

"What was that all about?"

"The cups check genetic compatibility. When a couple of different heritage contribute a DNA sample, the cup projects what characteristics the child would have."

Jerry looked deeply puzzled. "So you checked my DNA..."

"Against mine. Yes."

"Why?" Although he had a suspicion.

She looked at him sadly. "You really don't have any money, do you?"

"Not much." He thought of the few dollars left with his backpack in the copper room. "I have resources, as I said, but not enough money to buy a meal at this place."

She nodded. "Well, don't think too poorly of me, but I was out today hunting for a new boyfriend. I had hopes of finding someone who could afford to keep me here longer, so I wouldn't have to use my return ticket home. Hopefully someone who had the right DNA."

"What was wrong with the match?"

She looked at the cup. "As a hybrid, not much at all. He would have been healthy, smart and very, very pale, at least by the standards of my people. He would have been so pale that Sessi would burn him to death in a short time." She showed him the colorful pattern. "I wanted a black cup. An unviable match. I wanted no chance at all that an accident could happen." She looked at him, wistfully. "Do you understand?"

He nodded. "It wouldn't have worked anyway. I have someone else."

She nodded. "I could tell. But I have my pride. I might have been able to change your mind."

Nerib held her head high, "And I'm not destitute. Not yet. Get your temporary bank account set up and I'll give you enough cash to let you pay for a nice meal. Then you can treat me."

...

Lil added several tags to her ID number, "Lady Lillian, Lil, Lillian Nyson, Canton, Missouri, Earth, Doorway to Heaven, Copper Room." If she understood it right, searches wouldn't return names, but they might pick up the tags.

Next, she spent some time creating a custom call filter. "Reject everyone, except the ID's on my list and people whose search matches one of my ID tags and people who are over one thousand years old."

Seconds after she applied her call filter, an image of a man materialized across from the table from her. It was a still image, with his ID number and flags below. One of the flags read, "Bank of MH - Quality Control".

Uh, oh. She was in trouble.

"Hello?"

"Ah, you are there. I was happy to see my search for Lillian Nyson come up with a usable contact." It was still voice only, but the avatar image showed a nearly normal human male somewhere in his mid-twenties.

"This is Lillian. Is there a problem?"

"Possibly. The banking system constantly monitors the data that is entered into it, and sometimes, when information seems out of the normal, it flags a human to come and double-check its results. If you have time, would you mind a couple of questions about your account?"

"Okay. Go ahead."

"Our Banking regulations require me to state that the truthfulness of your answers will be checked via biometrics. Do you still want to answer?"

She sighed, "Yes." That was probably a lie, but there wasn't anything she could do about that.

"Hmm. It appears that your bank account is extremely old—possibly the oldest account in our records. However, the date of the account matches with the birthdate you have entered manually, which was...2,023 years ago?"

"That is correct. The birthdate and the account number I entered are correct."

There was a delay. "Okay. Remarkable, but I guess it had to happen eventually. It beats the previous record for long sleep by...well, that's not the bank's business.

"Okay, the other question is your planet of origin. You list 'Earth', which is probably your local name for it. Do you know the official designation?"

Lil frowned, trying to think. "No. I've always called it Earth. The birthplace of humanity? I've been...out of it for some time. I suppose you have a different name, but I don't know it."

"Okay. I'm sorry I don't have the historical resources to look that up. Well, I guess that's it. Thank you for your help and if there's anything..."

"Yes. I'm not the only one! Do you have another person my age that has recently shown up in your records? I came with a...partner."

The bank official paused again. "I am prohibited from giving out any information about any other person."

"Yes, you see, we got separated and this is quite a large place. I'm looking for him. Jereomy Harris?"

"I am very sorry about that. The Museum is overwhelming at first. And I'm sure you'll find your partner. Unfortunately, the regulations are very strict."

The call image collapsed. She wanted to call him back, to make another plea for information. His number was still in her call log, but she wasn't authorized to call it.

Oh Jerry, where are you?

...

"If I read the map correctly, I'm at the Haspen Concourse, on the base level."

The image of the gray-skinned and balding man with a bright red beard as his call avatar showed a frown. His voice seemed to imply that it might be his natural state.

"I know I haven't heard of you, and your ID doesn't match any of my students. If you're on this planet, why am I talking to you again?"

Jerry had teachers that had a similar distaste for talking to students out of class time. "I was searching for the expert on artifacts from G42-3."

His motives were simple. Information in this place cost money, and his remaining bank balance after Nerib said farewell and went off to find her a better companion, was barely enough to keep him fed for another day. If he were going to find Lil, he needed the goggle database system working for him, rather than putting up roadblocks every few seconds.

Other than romancing another girl for her money, which Lil wouldn't like at all, he needed to trade or sell something of value. And all of his valuables, including that stash of gold, were in the copper room.

Hiking back there without paying the access fee was officially theft of information, according to the Museum's rules. They had guards at the gateway. He'd risk it, but another way was to get a patron, a researcher, to let him in.

The red bearded man grumbled, "That's why you called me. But why should I spend my time talking to you?"

"Because I have unique information related to some of those artifacts. Information that was restricted even when I928734 was lifted from the planet and sent here."

Suddenly, the avatar switched to a live image of the man. He must have turned on a desk camera or something. "I wish I could see you. You sound too young to be a researcher."

"I'm not. I am just a person with direct experience."

He shook his head. "Not possible. That was an ancient automated light-sail ship. No crew. It practically disintegrated in space on the way here. We don't even have any records of why those artifacts were sent—other than they were the last shipment before the planet was put on the Black List, and that was maybe a thousand years ago. No person living knows."

Jerry felt his Lord Jereomy persona settling down on his shoulders. Who knew acting class would have so much effect on his life?

"I'm not of your time. Not of your culture, so bear with me. You are familiar with suspended animation, which allows people to sleep through long space flights?"

He snorted. "Of course. But no one..."

"There is more than one technology that can achieve the same effect."

He blinked. "Are you saying that you slept through a thousand years?"

Jerry paused for effect. "From my brief experience here at the Museum of Humanity, I've learned one thing. Information is the currency of this place. You can understand my hesitation in answering all questions in full.

"However, I will offer this, show me images of artifacts that were on that aging light-sail ship and I'll give you a brief identification of them."

When this researcher mentioned that the cargo consisted of artifacts from John's time, Jerry had been curious what they were. Maybe he wouldn't be able to identify anything, but if so, he still hadn't lost anything. The unnamed man didn't trust him yet.

He considered the offer. "Okay, I'll show you some of them."

His face moved to the side and a three dimensional image appeared in its place.

It was very familiar, from David's time.

"That is a 'machine gun'. As you can see, it is a tripod mounted weapon that fires pellets at high speed to kill and wound an enemy. The pellets are fired by an exploding gas contained in a small metal cylinder, one charge per pellet. The reaction from the force of the explosion advances a mechanism to place the next 'round' in position to be fired."

He wasn't really familiar with that individual weapon, but he knew the basics from his own time, and the magazine and barrel told the rest. Why this was considered an artifact worthy of being sent to the Museum of Humanity was a question on its own.

The next image appeared. From Meade's description, he knew it. "This is a segment from the 'Fallen Arch', originally it was an arch six hundred feet high above the banks of the Mississippi River at St. Louis Missouri in the United States of America. It was built as a monument to the western expansion of the settlers from the East Coast of the North American continent. In its interior, you can see remnants of a trolley system that carried passengers up to the view station at the peak of the arch.

"Sometime around the year 2200, a global catastrophe affected the planet and the arch fell. You can read names on the sides of this segment that were scratched in place after the fall."

The next image caught Jerry by surprise. As he moved his fingers in the air, rotating the three dimensional image, his brain was alive with speculation.

"Well, do you have anything to say about this box?"

"Yes, I do. I have seen it before, held by the man who built it. It appears to be a simple box with a latch, but it is frozen, impervious to any outside force. I do not know its history from then until now, but I do know how to open it."

The image vanished and the researcher's face took its place. "That's enough for now." He looked at something to the side, away from his desk camera. It was plain that what he'd heard had disturbed him.

Then, he looked back at the camera. "I'm satisfied. What do you want from me?"

. . .

The store clerk smiled at her. "I get that question quite a bit. The Museum is quite a mixing bowl of different cultures, and there's often confusion when it comes to marriage rules."

Looking around the shop had already led Lil to that conclusion. The place looked more like a cross between a sculptor's gallery and a Pier 1 Imports store than a bridal shop. The clerk stood behind a table of metal eggs.

"There are two kinds of marriages, a legal one, and a cultural one."

"What about a religious one?"

"That's part of the cultural side. For some, the religious aspects are the most important ones, but for others, the cultural side, religious and all, are ignored completely.

"The legal marriage, here in the Jen system and in fact for several light years around, consists of two parts." He picked up one of the metal eggs. "The egg, and the banking declaration."

His hand swept around the rest of the store. "But the cultural side is wide open, reflecting the traditions of the partners. We try to help out with all of the people who come to us, and our selection is very wide. We're also in contact with bridal shops in other concourses and can have other items we might not have here delivered in a matter of hours.

"What would you like?"

Lil looked again at all the statues and bowls and candles and ornate boxes. She'd already looked through the on-line catalog of wedding dresses. One could be built in the store in a matter of minutes, once her measurements were taken. Although the last wedding she'd attended was so far away in time and space that the catalog matched nothing she'd seen, she had no doubt that this place could produce a passable bridal veil if she needed one.

But there were no bridesmaids. There was no father to give her away, and no mother to cry. And no preacher to say the words.

She asked, "My religious tradition has a statement of principles and vows asked, given by a speaker. Do you have a way to contact someone like that? I haven't seen any religious advertisements."

The clerk nodded. "Of course! The advertising costs generally cause the holy leaders to rely on referrals and heavily targeted queries. But we have a list, specifically for those like you, who want a religious blessing for their wedding. Take a look at this." He held out an ornate silver tray, embossed with a pattern of dots. Instantly, a list of contacts appeared in the air before her. With growing confidence, she archived the list to her personal account.

"Perfect."

...

A melodious chime echoed through the Haspen Concourse. Jerry pulled out his cell phone and checked his time. The local hours were closer to the ones he'd grown up with than he had expected—about sixty-three minutes long. If it weren't for the timer running in the copper room, he would be able to use the new standard easily.

But it appeared that the day was winding down in the grand hallways of the Museum of Humanity. His appointment with Prime Researcher Matten was in the morning, and he hadn't thought to find a place to sleep for the night.

Where is Lil? This is the second night for her.

Unbidden, the thought that some guy might have offered her shelter, as Nerib had offered it to him, crept into his thoughts.

I should have found her by now. I should have gone with the flow of the traffic from the very beginning. That's what she must have done. But the map showed a dozen places, each as large as Haspen where she might have sought shelter.

It was even possible she had made her way back to the copper room, hiding in the dark places among the huge exhibits, wondering if he were ever going to come back.

She might even have made it all the way inside. Resting comfortably in their bed, having read the instruction sheet he'd left, explaining how the timer worked.

I wish I were there, in bed with her. But no, even that was a dead end. There was going to be little chance that they would ever hit the switch and leave all their troubles behind, wiped out by a few centuries. The Museum of Humanity had been here at least a thousand years, and should it ever cease operations, this would not be a place to be, underground inside a dead planet with a poisonous atmosphere. Jen-20 was a great place to build a museum for the ages, but not a happy place to be stranded.

They would have to find another solution.

Well, I'm working on it.

But there were more immediate problems.

He mumbled to the goggles, "Are there transient hostels, or homeless shelters within easy walking distance?"

A list appeared.

That one.

He should have expected it.

It was good to stretch his legs. He'd been sitting at tables most of the day. Part of the problem was that he'd been thinking of the concourse as a shopping mall, when it was really a neighborhood. There were more than restaurants. There were residences, gymnasiums, exercise courts, parks, a wide variety of stores, a library, and even a few churches.

He walked into the door marked with the simple cross. A man with pale green hair draped to his shoulders looked up. "Can I help you?"

It was embarrassing. He didn't like to ask for help. But, he'd done it before, and Speaker Joseph hadn't bitten his head off.

"Unfortunately, yes. I'm a new arrival, and I've messed up my arrangements. Is there a place I could spend the night?"

There was. He was given a blanket and a narrow bed among a half-dozen others. The rules of the house were listed.

"Thank you. By the way, is there a list of people who have lost contact with each other? I'm searching for a Lillian Nyson."

...

She smiled at the avatar with the Christian cross icon in the background. "Thanks again for your advice. I'll be sure to give you a call back when we've made final arrangements."

"I'm glad to help. The ceremony you describe is a bit more ornate than what we usually have in this place, but that may be because so many of the girls are here alone, with their parents much too far away to be here in person."

Lil sighed. "My parents are long gone. And I don't mean to suggest that I'd want the whole thing I described. Probably the ceremony you're used to performing would be better."

"I'm sure you'll need to discuss it with your fiancee, too."

She nodded. "That reminds me. I hate to admit it, but I've misplaced him. Do you have a database where I could list him, in case he asks? I'm looking for Jereomy Harris."

...

Jerry had stretched out in the darkened room, and realized that he was still wearing the goggles. The designer had done a good job of making them nearly weightless and invisible, when not shining advertisements into your eyes. He thought about taking them off, in case he rolled over in the night. He was about to act on it when the call came through.

"Lil!"

"Jerry! I thought I'd never find you again."

He hopped up and stepped out into the hallway so he could speak louder.

"I am so relieved. You have a safe place to stay for the night?"

"Yes, I made a friend. She's putting me up until I find you."

A lead weight dropped away as one worry vanished.

"I'm at a church shelter. Listen. I have a very important meeting scheduled in the morning. Do you have the resources to buy an access ticket to Great Hall 9?"

...

Two hours later, Mary came home to find Lil giggling and mumbling to someone in her goggles, curled up around a pillow on the couch and looking as happy as she'd ever been.

Jerry was content to sleep in his goggles, once he learned to turn up the sound and listen to her breathing. Some time in the night, he actually slept.

...

He was first in line at the gateway to the Great Hall, impatiently waiting for the official opening just to confirm that his red bearded patron had cleared his access. He didn't try to run the whole distance back, but the walk that had taken an hour yesterday was completed in half the time.

As he walked up to the Doorway to Heaven, or 1928734 as the goggles had it listed, there was only a minimal listing for customers displayed on the walls. Depending on how the day went, that could easily change. Keeping the copper room a personal secret was no longer part of his plans.

There was no bench or seating of any kind at this station, although he had seen plenty near more popular exhibits. He settled down where he could keep a constant eye out. When the parade of spectators began passing his way, and he began attracting too much attention, he relocated to a position in the rear where he wouldn't be as visible.

The copper room's color flickered slightly, and then again a minute later. Jerry resisted the impulse to make a dash for the doorway. He checked his cell phone clock. The time had drifted two minutes. He made the mental correction and sat back down to wait.

. . .

Lil was angry. "What do you mean it will take me four hours to get there? I started there, and it didn't take me that long to get here!"

The gateway guard had seen too many upset students to be bothered. "It's a one-way access. You have to go up to the Fine Art Causeway and then back down the Grand Hall. I don't make the rules. There's so much traffic that I can't make exceptions just for you."

"Look mister, I have people waiting for me, and I don't have a lot of time."

He shrugged and turned to deal with a bus approaching the access.

She called Jerry.

"Trouble at the main gate. I can't get a fast route to the Doorway. They say four hours."

"Hmm. I can't wait that long. My guy is due here in an hour, and if I don't produce, then I'm out of luck, out of money, and out of ideas."

"Go on without me. I'll get there as fast as I can."

He sighed. "Okay, but it would go smoother with you to help."

"It's okay. Lord Jereomy can pull it off. You always do."

She closed the call and started looking around.

"Are there high speed tours?" she asked.

A list appeared. She turned and sprinted, as well as she could in her long white dress, down the concourse. Advertisements listed prices as well. She would have to sell something to make it work.

. . .

Jerry was waiting as a utility vehicle moved up in the fast lane past the latest group of students and pulled in at 1928734. He checked his phone clock.

Prime Matten, who was nearly as tall as he was, stepped out carrying the box.

Jerry held out his hand. "I am Jereomy Harris."

He set the box down on the ground. "I am Timethus Matten, Prime Researcher." He hesitated over the handshake. It obviously wasn't his practice.

"Are you ready?"

"In five minutes or so."

"I do want to warn you, that I have already logged this activity with the Board. If you try anything irregular, if you harm the box, there will be severe consequences."

Jerry smiled. "Do you actually think I can harm the box?"

He didn't answer.

Off in the distance, there was a shout. "Jerry!"

Speeding up on one of the surfboard things, Lil was racing his way, her skirt flapping in the breeze.

"Ah. Here is my associate."

The researcher frowned, "The one you wanted me to find?"

"Yes. You're off the hook for that part of our deal."

Lil stepped off the board and ran up to her fiancee, bare feet flying. They hugged. She whispered. "I had to sell my shoes, and now I'm flat broke."

"It won't matter in two minutes," he whispered back.

She nodded and walked on past, though their fingers were the last to part.

"I'm ready now. Give me the box."

Timethus handed it over. "I think it may contain books or something with that density. That's all I have been able to determine."

"We'll find out." Jerry moved quickly toward the iron door.

"What are you doing?"

"You want it open. I have to use tools that are inside."

"But the doorway to the metal room is just as frozen as the box!"

Jerry nodded, "Exactly."

Timethus began to follow, but the color flickered and Lil shoved the door open and was in. Jerry sprinted the remaining ten feet and followed. The researcher followed, but the door shut before he could reach it.

...

Lil flipped the switch. "I've suspended them."

"You set it like we discussed?"

She pointed at the dial. It was set at the 3600X mark. "What's this all about?"

He set the box down on the table.

"This is Uncle Greg's time demo box. It's the same thing as the copper room, only smaller. He took it with him on a trip when we had our accident. It has been time-frozen for two thousand years as well, probably kicking around in one museum or research laboratory or another. And look here." He pointed at the top lid.

Scratched into the metal were numbers. 1/3600X

"What's that?"

"I have to think Uncle Greg left it for me, for us, with some clue as to how to open it. A clue that we could use, but not anyone else. When I saw it in Timethus Matten's list of items that rode across space with us, I saw this code and knew I had to try it."

"We're at the 3600X speed, moving faster than the outside," she said. "So you think it's at the other 3600X speed, moving slower?"

"That's all I can guess. Let's see if it opens." He pressed the latch, but it didn't budge.

"Problem?"

He frowned. "Maybe it has to be in contact with the walls."

He walked it over to the doorway's frame, where bare metal was exposed. He pressed it tightly to the metal.

"If this doesn't work, I'll have to do some fancy explaining when we go back outside."

"Jerry! Look!" The color shifted.

"Open it. I've got to use both hands to hold it in place."

Lil flipped the latch easily. The instant the lid opened up, she saw the switch—like a wind-up timer, and turned it off.

"That did it." He carried the box back to the table. "Let's see what Uncle Greg left us."

...

"Greetings, Jereomy and Lillian.

"I had hoped to meet you in person one day and to apologize for letting you fall into this trap. I hope you will forgive me for leaving so dangerous a situation unsecured.

"I want you to know that I struggled for decades to find a way to reverse the controls from outside the room. It is a painful irony that I have learned the secret, only too late to do anything about it. My health is failing and although I have been made wealthy selling a handful of 'study rooms', ones with only one set of controls, to select customers, I no longer have the strength, nor any trusted aides to help me do more than put this box together.

"It is my hope that when you recover from your fall and turn off the time field you will notice that the grandfather clock just outside the door is resting on a pedistal and discover this box hidden inside clamped to the wall.

"I used extremely slow sound waves to map the interior of the copper room and saw the two of you and understand that you fell against the controls by accident.

"In here is a history from when you went into the room until now. There is an instruction manual that details the changes I made to the house to supply your short term needs for power and water, as well as how to access an underground store room with other materials you might need.

"In addition, there are two pads, with greetings from your respective families. Over the decades, the Harris and Nyson clans have gone from bitter enemies to fast friends. The sonogram showing you two together and proving that it was an accident did much to heal the anger and suspicion that arose from your disappearance.

"My will has left the house and grounds and the copper room by name to a foundation whose purpose is to turn the assets over to you. Full instructions are included.

"This is all I have been able to do to make amends for what I have done. I hope for forgiveness.

"Greg Montain"

. . .

Lil had been reading over his shoulder, and before he finished, she dug into the box and pulled out a pad with her name on it.

She pressed a button, and her mother appeared on the screen. "Hello, Lil. They say you'll be able to see this some day, so I want to tell you how much I love you."

It was just the first clip of many. Apparently, the idea of sending a care package through time had started early, for it was an annual event. In short, three minute clips, she watched her sister grow up, and her parents grow old. She watched nieces and nephews, birthdays and graduations.

"Honey," her father said in a clip he'd plainly recorded in the middle of some sleepless night, "I know you care for this guy, but please play it safe."

Her ears burned hot as she suffered through an honest father-daughter talk about sex and its consequences. She loved him for it.

. . .

The Harris family had suffered. His parents had split and there were few greetings beyond a couple of arranged meetings to record words of love and hopes for his future.

So, I had a step brother, twenty years younger than me. I wonder what happened to him.

Uncle Greg had remained a hermit scientist, in spite of the growing signs of his wealth. Jerry's pad also contained details about the time mechanism, and a copy of the sonogram video, taken over the course of several years, that showed him falling after Lil had knocked him down. Just a fraction of a second of their long journey through time, but it had been enough to tell everything about Lil's feelings for him.

. . .

Lil held the pad to her chest. She looked him in the eye. "Thank you, for this."

"It was all Uncle Greg. We were supposed to find the box that first stop, but looters had already ransacked the house by then and had ripped it all out. I wonder what was in that underground store room we never found."

"It doesn't matter. Jerry, you know what this is?" she held the pad. "No."

"It's my parents blessing, on us, on our marriage. I think that was the last thing that had been nagging at me."

He nodded. In a lesser way, his folks had done the same.

She smiled, timidly, "I have something for us."

"Oh?"

She held out a metal egg. "Do you know what this is?"

He strained to keep a grin off his face. "Ah, sort of. A DNA test? Right?"

She looked at him sternly. "I can tell you have a story, but later. It's a part of a marriage, in the here and now. It separates into two little cups. We each take a sip and mix the results. Our genetic compatibility is shown on the side of the cup and if we agree, we press here and the results are sent to the central registry.

"I was told that often, the cup turns black when variants from widely different backgrounds are tested, which means no children. Mostly dark gray means the children would be deformed or defective in other ways and mandatory counseling is required of couples who face that situation.

"Many times, black or gray puts a stop to the idea of marriage at all."

He put his arm around her. "It's not likely that we would have any problem. You don't need to worry."

"So are you ready for this step?"

He nodded. "I am, but we can't do it here." He gestured around at the walls. "Metal room. Even at normal time, the radio waves can't get through. But definitely later today, once we get rid of the researcher."

She elbowed him in the ribs. "But no waffling." She nodded toward their bed. "I've been ready. I am ready. Waiting will be hard."

He kissed her with a sincerity that settled any doubts.

. . .

"Lil, I made a deal. I would open the box, and in exchange Matten will smooth the way for us in this world. I have to go back outside and give him the box and what it contains."

She looked horrified, clutching the pad with all her family's videos.

He nodded, "But plainly not the original contents. Surely we can make up a replacement for him?"

They emptied the box and Jerry put several books inside, including John's book of legends.

"Several of those were getting rare when I checked them out of the library. They ought to be unique in this era."

Lil offered her economics text and her cheerleader's playbook. "Just to give the social anthropologists something to play with."

Jerry chuckled. "Be sure you keep all your photos and videos safe. All of those are valuable historical artifacts as well."

"I think I'll hang onto my phone for a little bit longer."

He nodded. "At least until we've learned this era's tech."

Jerry took a knife and carefully unscrewed the time control circuit in the little box. Filled with books, there was little sign that it had been there.

"There's a chance we won't be able to come back in, once he realizes the door to the room can be opened. Pack your bags."

Lil frowned, "Didn't your uncle say you inherited this place?"

"Yes, but other than the papers here in the box, there's no proof."

"You might be surprised. Did you reactivate your original Missouri bank account?"

"No. Is that even possible?"

...

Two seconds after the iron door had shut in his face, it opened back up and Jerry came out, carrying the open box. Timethus Matten's momentary suspicion was overwhelmed by the sight of the books. Jerry stared off in space, mumbling a couple of times as the researcher pulled special gloves from his truck and began pulling the books one at a time out of the box.

Lil tapped Jerry on the shoulder and nodded. He took a deep breath and walked over to the man hunched over the ancient volumes. He watched until the man started carefully turning the pages in John's book.

"That book is a thousand years old, the others are all twice that age. All preserved by that technology I mentioned.

"Of course, you realize that the copper room, all its contents, and this box and its contents are my property."

"What? No! The Museum has title to everything here."

Jerry leaned against the truck. "Oh, I'm sure it will have to be adjudicated, but the fact remains that I have original documentation showing my ownership, plus I can prove that I've held possession of the copper room for the entire two thousand years since its construction. You can't claim a space ship in flight just because its crew are in long sleep, can you? The copper room is my time ship! The Museum may have transported it, but we were inside the whole time. It never gained a title superior to mine."

The man appeared horrified, and Jerry suspected from his mumbles, that he was researching the title as they spoke. But he had filed his claim moments ago.

He held up his hand. "Now, I don't mean to cut you out of anything. I'm sure we can work out a joint access arrangement. I need your help, but you also need mine." He pointed at John's book. "You need the help of Lord Jereomy and Lady Lillian."

...

Matten didn't push trying to get into the copper room once he realized that it was again frozen solid.

"How did you do that?"

Jerry shrugged. "My ship, as I said. It's a special lock. Don't worry, if things go smoothly, I'll let you in soon enough."

He loaded the box of ancient books into his truck as soon as Jerry confirmed that the other arrangements had been completed.

Lil watched him go with a sigh of relief. "So we have a place to stay?"

"And two fully paid research assistantships, for a couple of years at least. I think, now that we're out of high school, that maybe we should get our college degrees? This is supposedly the best school available. You did want to go to some place other than your home town college, didn't you?"

She smiled. "I'm comfortable here. With the translator goggles, we won't have to learn a new language. I was worried about that. Are you sure you won't have the itch to move on?"

He laughed, "Not without you, and a real space ship. But I am a little curious about what happened to the Earth. Of course, that would take more money. Everything we own, books, laptops, clothes, are valuable antiques, but for a space ship, I'd have to dangle the time circuitry."

"That's valuable?"

"Really valuable. Their interstellar economy is built on slow starships and medically induced comas. It's safe enough for a couple of dozen years, but after that, complications and even fatalities start to make it more difficult. A hundred-year sleep is rare. I think about three hundred and fifty is the record."

Lil mentioned her banker's call. "So a thousand-year sleep is amazing."

"We can change all that. Replace a medical coma with the flip of a switch, and with no limit to how long it lasts. It's valuable. If we can avoid being tricked out of it, we shouldn't have to worry about money."

She leaned against him. "On another note, I think it's your time to pay up." She slipped her fingers between the buttons of his shirt.

"I'm ready." He looked back at the room as the time-lock expired. They'd set it to only stay locked long enough to get rid of the researcher.

She pulled out the egg and mumbled a few words. After a moment, she asked, "Are you ready there, Mary, and Su Parmer?"

The preacher and her maid of honor appeared in the air as goggle images. The joint banking account had been registered. All that remained were the egg and the words.

The ceremony was surprisingly normal, from Jerry's perspective. The preacher asked them to vow fidelity to each other and asked the blessings of heaven on their union.

Instead of a ring ceremony, Lil poured some water into the two cups and they sipped and as the colored bars appeared, Jerry and Lil noticed that several bystanders had bailed out of the passing parade to watch.

They logged their compatibility to the central registry, and the preacher pronounced them married.

The top rim of each of the cups peeled off and Lil and Jerry slipped them on as self adjusting arm bands, the current culture's version of a wedding ring.

The spectators congratulated them and Lil said goodbye to their official witnesses.

Jerry tilted his head toward the iron door. She nodded and they slipped inside. The strangers barely realized what had happened when the door opened again.

He had changed back to his original clothes, with letter jacket and jeans. Lil was in her cheerleader outfit and her face glowed. She appeared permanently attached to his side. They pulled out their bags and closed the iron door behind them.

"Are you people still here?" he said with a big smile. "We're done. You can leave now." There was good natured laughter. The room flickered in color as they loaded their bags onto Lil's surfboard and they sped off to their new home.

The End

Henry Melton is often on the road with his wife Mary Ann, a nature photographer. From the Redwood forests to Death Valley to the Great Lakes

to Delaware swamps to the African bush, scenes out the windshield become locales for his fiction work. He is frequently captivated by the places he visits, and that has inspired a wonderful series of novels; **Small Towns, Big Ideas**. Check his website, *HenryMelton.com* for current location, his stories, a blog of his activities, and scheduled appearances. Henry's short fiction has been published in many magazines and anthologies, most frequently in Analog. Catacomb, published in Dragon magazine, is considered a classic

Many titles, and more are coming. This series that appeals to age 12 and up by Henry Melton is available now. Starting in the here and now, these tales follow the trials of high school aged heros that take that extra step into the fantastic when something unexpected drops into their lives. Many of the classic science fiction ideas like teleportation, alien contact and time travel are explored in a way totally accessible to many readers who "don't read that kind of stuff" as well as being an exciting adventure for those who do. Available as paper and e-books on-line everywhere.

Falling Bakward

by Henry Melton
ISBN 978-0-9802253-6-5
ePub ISBN 978-1-935236-24-5
Kindle ISBN 978-1-935236-14-6

Jerry Ingram wanted to be special, more than just a sixth-generation farmer in South Dakota and spent hours after school digging at the mystery spot in the back fields, searching for Indian artifacts. With Sheriff Musgrave always picking on his family and Dad always worried about money, an important discovery would be a great lift. But those bones he found weren't Indian, and when a cave-in drove him into the metal craft buried since the last ice age he found a portal to the world of the Bak, and discovered that the gentle, zebra-striped giants had been waiting for his family for thousands of years!

...

"...just about everyone in Jerry's family has secrets...the story flows well and is easy to follow. The Bak are an engaging race, and the Kree are suitably terrifying. I can almost see this as a '50s monster movie, but with much better characterization. Lots of thrills, plenty of suspense, and widescreen action... If you're looking for YA science fiction in the sense-of-wonder vein, check out Falling Bakward." Bill Crider, author of the Sheriff Dan Rhodes series, among many other things. *3/15/09*

"His writing style is much like that of Robert A. Heinlein and Isaac Asimov when they were writing what was known at the time as Juvenile Fiction...a satisfying read for adults as well... It was quite awhile before I put it down again and then only reluctantly." Elizabeth J. Baldwin, author of Horses *3/10/09*

Lighter Than Air

by Henry Melton
ISBN 978-0-9802253-1-0
ePub ISBN 978-1-935236-23-8
Kindle ISBN 978-1-935236-13-9

Winner of the 2009 Eleanor Cameron / Golden Duck Award

It could be the best prank in the history of Munising High School's unof-

ficial Prank Day. Working for a next door neighbor inventor had left Jon Kish with unlimited quantities of lighter-than-air foam, perfect for building... say, a full-sized flying saucer! High school honor demanded it. Plus with the family stress of his mother's surgery, he needed something to keep his mind occupied. But little sister Cherry had her own schemes in play, and events more serious than high school pranks or Mother's cancer were about to focus the world's attention on this little northern town.

...

"Lighter Than Air is a good read for the whole family that teenagers will love from start to finish! Ample scientific facts are scattered throughout the story, thus enriching the plot and feeding the mind. It is entertaining and exciting to read" Liana Metal, Midwest Book Review 12/2008

"Melton weaves a tale of secrets and suspense, science and pranks, emotion and intrigue...the tedium of the scientific jargon is minimalized by Melton's exquisite ability to tell a story...the scene where Jon and his friend and co-conspirator, Larry, unleash their UFO on an unsuspecting Halloween Festival crowd is priceless. The scary part of the story, though, is not how the characters deal with the issue of death, but that of Internet predators...I found the possibility all too real, and you might as well." Benjamin Potter, October 13, 2008

Extreme Makeover

by Henry Melton
ISBN 978-0-9802253-2-7
ePub ISBN 978-1-935236-22-1
Kindle ISBN 978-1-935236-12-2

Lightning brought a towering redwood crashing down around her, and something dripped on her skin. After that, high school senior Deena Brooke struggled to make sense of the impossible changes to her body. She was grateful for the interest Luther Jennings had in her puzzling insights and quirky urges, until she discovered that he was hiding a deadly secret of his own. Alien nanobots had invaded her body, an unseen influence that was changing her into something else! And was Luther helping her or dragging her into some criminal scam of his own?

...

"I've recently read the #1 best-selling YA novel, and Henry's is much better written. It's also better paced and has a better story and better-realized characters. Trust me." Bill Crider, Author of the Sheriff Dan Rhodes series and others. 10/08/08

"The plot is quite tight and believable, and so are the characters. They are 'real' kids with their own family problems who try to solve the riddle of Deena's sudden change. It is a very exciting story from the very first page to the last one." Liana Metal, Midwest Book Review September 2008

"Once in awhile you read something that is really fun. If you pick up a Henry Melton book that's what you'll find...this is a superb example of young adult science fiction." Benjamin Potter, August 11, 2008

Roswell or Bust

by Henry Melton

ISBN 978-0-9802253-0-3

ePub ISBN 978-1-935236-21-4

Kindle ISBN 978-1-935236-11-5

Teenager Joe Ferris was raised to help guests -- he was third generation in his family's motel business -- but once he connected with mute Judith, they were off on an epic thousand mile road trip through the Southwest, all to help the most unique guests of all -- the Roswell aliens stranded far from home since 1947. With the Men in Black hot on their trail, and discovering that the aliens had more tricks up their sleeves than their captors had ever discovered, Joe and Judith have to wonder just who is taking whom on the ride of their lives!

...

"Reading Roswell or Bust will let you enjoy Science Fiction, even if you haven't been a big fan in the past, and will clue you into why Melton was chosen for an award from the SF community in his first outing as a novelist. It's a great escape (and not only for the aliens who've been kept captive for many decades) Benjamin Potter, April 7, 2008

"The plot is tight... A strange talkie, a mysterious courier and a couple of spies are all involved in this exciting story that will entertain kids of that age... It caters to all the family." Liana Metal, Midwest Book Review July 2008

"...whimsically amusing. The story inside is a wonderful read...His characters are real, complete with the small concerns and everyday trials...adventures are zany and compelling, keeping the reader enthralled to the end when the book can be closed with satisfaction." Ethan Rose, coauthor of Rowan of the Wood

Emperor Dad

by Henry Melton
ISBN 978-0-9802253-4-1
ePub ISBN 978-1-935236-20-7
Kindle ISBN 978-1-935236-10-8

Winner of the 2008 Darrell Award for Best Novel.

His dad was up to something, but it wasn't until James Hill saw the theft of the British Crown Jewels live on CNN and the bizarre claims of this new Emperor of the Earth, did he realize Dad might have invented teleportation in the shed in the back yard. Bob Hill had a plan to protect the world from his disruptive invention, but when the police forces of the world move in on him, no one knew James had hacked the family computer and had taken the power of teleportation himself. Now only he could save his family, and the world.

...

"It follows in the best tradition of other juvenile SF/action adventure novels in that it follows a young man trying to solve the usual problems that confront any young man (the search for self-identity, relationships with girls, family, and society) at the same time as he must solve the larger problems that surround him (such as whether his father is a mysterious shadowy figure branded as a global terrorist, and what to do when FBI agents show up at the door)... great job of balancing suspense and humor...no real belly laughs, but there were quite a lot of chuckles." Chris Meadows, Teleread January 7th, 2009

"It's a fast-moving SF adventure that's a lot of fun ... Cool cover." Bill Crider -- August 1, 2007

"I had a blast reading this book! With every page turned, you don't want it to end." J. Stock August 16, 2007

Golden Girl

by Henry Melton
ISBN 978-0-9802253-5-8
ePub ISBN 978-1-935236-25-2
Kindle ISBN 978-1-935236-15-3

Debra Barr was barely out of bed when she found herself thrust into a pivotal role in the future of the human race. Plucked out of her bedroom in small town Oquawka, Illinois to a future Earth destroyed and poisoned by a major asteroid impact, the future scientists explained how she could walk a few steps differently, and with YouTube, save the planet. But everything they told her was wrong. Instead of returning to her bedroom, she appeared two hundred years in the past, and it was up to her to discover the rules of time travel without killing herself. Bouncing through time, only one thing was certain, anything she decided to do could mean life or death for her family and friends and the route she chose would likely cost her everything. Unfortunately, the more she discovered, the more she suspected that everyone was lying to her.

...

Not Your Usual Time Travel Story

"Stories that give serious consideration to the issues of paradox and causality in time travel are few and far between. But Henry Melton's latest young-adult book, Golden Girl, is one that treats time travel the right way. It starts from an interesting premise, adds a unique time travel mechanic, and puts a teenaged girl at the center of an interesting dilemma—with nothing less than the survival of the entire human race at stake!

One of the things I have always enjoyed about Henry Melton's books is that they feature intelligent, self-reliant teens who are by and large able to solve their own problems. There is nothing juvenile in how these young-adult novels are put together. Henry Melton is a master storyteller, and I will be anxiously awaiting his next work."

Chris Meadows TeleRead

Follow That Mouse

by Henry Melton

ISBN 978-0-9802253-7-2

ePub ISBN 978-1-935236-28-3

Kindle ISBN 978-1-935236-18-4

Dot Comal loved her home town, although the Utah ranching community of Ranch Exit was too small to call a 'town'. She had her horse, Pokey, and her father to care for, and Ned from the next ranch over was comfortable to be around when he showed up on his motorcycle. But things were changing. The animals, and even her father, were showing signs of a growing irrational rage. Only Watson Winekia, the old Paiute shaman claimed any knowledge of what was happening, but he was too old and he expected Dot to heal the valley. She was at a loss, until a strange mouse led her to bigger secrets than she'd ever imagined, hidden below her feet. She had to wield mysteries hidden for decades quickly, before her home town and everything she loved was wiped off the map!

...

"The plot was very unique and mind-boggling. Although it is sci-fi, it didn't feel extremely fantastical or out there because it had a realistic set up. Dot's world didn't change overnight, but there were signs and clues which foreshadowed a bigger-than-her conflict."(: ISA :) mixturesbooks.blogspot.com

"Follow that Mouse is sprinkled with interesting, seemingly factual info, while the mysterious impression of odd events turns more serious and gives way to a gripping, constantly evolving (literally!) story that is both intelligent and thought-provoking, disturbing and startling in its revelations. Ned and Dot's relationship is comfortable and real, and the revealed villain has a classic, yet distinctive and creative feel to it - not in a comical sense, to be clear, as this villain is BAD. This is a truly unpredictable, refreshing, and super smart YA sci-fi/fantasy novel that is entertaining, and at the same time expects you to exercise your brain. Follow that Mouse is surprising right up to the end, and keeps you guessing just as long. I highly recommend it!!!"

Angie L Bibliophilesupportgroup.

Bearing Northeast

by Henry Melton
ISBN 978-0-9802253-9-6
ePub ISBN 978-1-935236-29-0
Kindle ISBN 978-1-935236-19-1

Rule 1: We'll always be Brother and Sister...

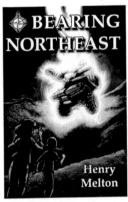

A mysterious metal cylinder falling out of the sky was the perfect excuse to take a vacation when sixteen year old Seth Parmer and Biz, his older sister and sometimes 'parent' found their Fresno lives upended by her unexpected layoff. With Seth's twitter buddies following along on his phone, a GPS tracking signal leads them from California across the continent toward a hidden project in the desolate lands in the middle of Labrador. The electric secret they find there will not only forge a new global destiny for the unique town that they discover, but set a new course for their relationship with each other.

Pack your ice chest, charge your cell phone and bring your maps, as Henry Melton, award winning author of Emperor Dad and Lighter Than Air, takes you on a trek to a place in the far north where a high school science club is reaching for the sky.

Pixie Dust

by Henry Melton
ISBN 978-0-9802253-8-9
ePub ISBN 978-1-935236-27-6
Kindle ISBN 978-1-935236-17-7

Jenny Quinn's life was on course for her advanced physics degree until a lab experiment in vacuum decay turned her life upside down. With career hopes destroyed and her professor dead in an unexplained fall, she is forced to cope with a strange change in her own body. With nothing but her own resources, a childhood infatuation with old comic books may be her only guide to help solve the twin mysteries of cutting edge physics and the murder of her professor, before one or the other puzzle gets her killed.

Henry Melton, award winning author of the YA adventures Emperor Dad and Lighter Than Air, takes us on an adventure with a slightly older heroine, even if she is just four foot ten and everyone calls her Tinkerbell.

The PROJECT Saga

Beginning a new multivolume storyline of human destiny that spans thousands of years where planets are moved and worlds are shaped.

Star Time

by Henry Melton
ISBN 978-1-935236-30-6
ePub ISBN 978-1-935236-31-3
Kindle ISBN 978-1-935236-32-0

It all starts here...

The plan always worked for the bloodthirsty Cerik, whose battle-bred claws and muscles made them the uncontested top preda-tor on scores of planets–the radiation pulse from the supernova would turn civilization on the blue-white globe below into chaos within days, making for easy prey.

In Texas, in a wooden cabin where she'd hidden from regular humans since birth, telepathic Sharon Dae knew nothing could prevent humanity from becoming another tasty slave race–she'd read it plainly from the thoughts in the sky. A scout ship had crashed in her woods, but these alien Hunt-ers would vaporize thousands just to keep any human prey from the frag-ments. She sensed a stranger, Abe Whiting nearby, hunting for debris with his computers and gadgets. Painfully, she realized she would have to learn how to lie and betray to get the prize away from him, even if she couldn't escape the jaws of the Cerik herself. How could she know that this techno wizard would soon brave the collapse of the world, cobbling together fried scraps and pieces in an impossible rescue attempt for her, a strange white-haired trickster of a girl who slipped through his life for only one afternoon?

It all starts here, the first installment of a multi-volume, multi-thousand year tale of human destiny from the mind of Henry Melton.

CPSIA information can be obtained at www.ICGtesting.com
Printed in the USA
LVOW080445261111

256537LV00001B/7/P

9 781935 236337